DISTRACTIONS

The race reality never wins

by

BRIAN B. TURNER

DISTRACTIONS

Copyright © 2026 by Brian B. Turner

This is a work of fiction. Names, characters, places, events, and dialogues are products of the author's imagination. Any resemblance to actual persons, living or dead, or actual events is entirely coincidental.

For permissions requests, inquiries, or more information, contact:

HEY BBT LLC Publishing
www.heybbt.com

ISBN: 978-1-971050-03-4

Printed in the United States of America

First Edition

Table of Contents

Chapter One: The Life That Did Not Fit

Kai woke before the alarm, the way people do when something inside them stirs first.

For a moment, he did not move.
He lay still, listening to a silence that felt like it was listening back.
Nothing was wrong.
Nothing was different.
Yet the room felt borrowed, as if he were waking up in someone else's morning.

He sat up slowly.

The air carried a slight unfamiliarity, the kind you notice only when the world is one degree off its usual shape.
Light fell across the walls in a pattern he did not recognize.

On the dresser stood a framed photo of him on a beach.

He picked it up.

He had never been to that beach.

The man in the photo looked like him. Same shoulders. Same half smile. Same quiet posture.

But the memory was not his.
Not even faintly.

He set the frame down with the careful touch you give something that feels true and false at the same time.

The house was quiet.
Not peaceful.
Not heavy.
Just paused.
Like the morning was waiting for him to notice something.

He walked to the kitchen.
The clock above the sink blinked 6:02, steady and indifferent.
On the counter sat a mug with a chipped handle.

He did not own a mug with a chipped handle.

A soft ache rose in his chest. Not fear. Not confusion. Recognition.

It felt like waking up in a life meant for someone else.

He sensed, in a small, quiet place inside him, that he had been here before without ever living it.

He felt an odd pull in his chest, the kind that comes when your mind is trying to remember something your life has not lived yet.

His phone buzzed on the table.
A message appeared from a contact named Mira.

Hope you slept. We need to talk.

The name did not match any memory he carried.
Yet somewhere quiet inside him, beneath thought,
it felt familiar enough to unsettle him.

He looked around the room again.
Same light.
Same furniture.
Same morning.

Yet none of it felt like home.

Kai steadied his hands against the counter. Not
from panic. From clarity.

The world around him had not changed.

Only the version of him standing in it.

He felt the room waiting for him, as if it knew
something he did not.

He stood there for a moment, hand on the
doorframe, unsure why crossing into the morning
felt like stepping into a memory he did not own.

Kai stepped outside, hoping the morning air would
settle whatever had shifted inside him.
The light touched the street in its usual way, gentle

and unhurried, yet something about it felt slightly unfamiliar.
Not brighter.
Not dimmer.
Simply different, as if the morning had remembered something he had forgotten.

He walked toward the driveway.

Across the street, a woman waved.
Her smile was soft, the kind people use when they trust the history between you.
She said his name with the ease of routine.

Good morning, Kai.

He lifted his hand out of courtesy, though he had never seen her in his life.
Her familiarity pressed against him like a memory that did not belong to him.

He reached his car.
Except it was not his car.
Same model. Same color.
A slight change in the trim.
A quiet difference only someone who lived with the car would notice.

Even the air felt misaligned, holding warmth where the morning should have been cool.

He touched the door handle.
It felt like touching a moment from someone else's past.

For a moment, he sensed he was not alone, the kind of awareness that arrives before the mind understands why.

A voice spoke behind him.

Morning.

Kai turned.

A man stood on the sidewalk.
Older.
Calm eyes.
A presence that felt anchored in a world Kai no longer recognized.

The man looked at him with a steady patience.

You alright? You look like someone who woke up in the wrong story.

Kai tried to answer, but the words stayed behind his breath.
He did not know how to explain a feeling he did not yet understand.

The man nodded, as if Kai's silence confirmed something.

Happens more often than people admit.

He continued walking down the street.
No urgency.
No curiosity.

As if he had simply delivered a truth that did not require a reaction.

Kai watched him disappear around the corner.

He opened the car door.
The interior smelled faintly of a place he could not name.
The seats were worn in patterns that belonged to someone else's life.
A single key rested in the cup holder.
Not his key.
Not his history.

He sat inside and glanced at the rearview mirror.

His reflection stared back.
Same face.
Same eyes.
Yet behind them was a quiet vacancy, as if a small part of him had stayed behind in the life he remembered.

His phone vibrated.
The message from Mira glowed again.

Hope you slept. Please call me. We need to talk.

He closed his eyes for a moment.

The world had not broken.
It had not shifted in anger or chaos.
It had shifted in silence, almost politely, into a life that was not his.

He opened his eyes.

Everything looked the same.

Which was the clearest sign that nothing was.

Something in him understood that whatever had shifted was not finished with him yet.

He wondered if the world was changing or if he was finally noticing what had already begun.

Chapter Two: Familiar but Wrong

Kai stayed in the car a moment longer, letting the quiet sit with him. The morning waited outside the window, steady and unchanged, as if the world refused to acknowledge anything unusual.

He took a slow breath and stepped out.
The gravel under his feet felt familiar.
The feeling inside him did not.

He could feel his mind reaching for a memory that refused to arrive, a silence where certainty should have been.

His phone buzzed again.
Mira calling.

He stared at the name, hoping for recognition that did not arrive.
He answered anyway.

You left early. Her voice was calm, almost gentle.
Have you been up long?

Kai swallowed. Not long.

There was a pause on her end. The kind of pause where someone is trying to read your silence.

You sound off. Everything alright?

He looked at the house.
At the unfamiliar car.
At the street that felt like a memory someone had
painted over.

I am fine, he said. Just tired.

Another pause.

You are never tired in the mornings.

The sentence felt precise, like someone placing a
puzzle piece where it belonged.
Except that the picture he completed was not his.

Mira exhaled softly.

I can come by if you want. We were supposed to talk
last night, remember.

He closed his eyes.
A small, quiet ache formed in his chest.
Something about her voice moved through him
with a familiarity he did not understand.

He opened his eyes again.

I do not remember last night, he said.

Silence on the line.
Not angry.
Not confused.
Just still.

Finally, she spoke.

Kai, you forget things when you get overwhelmed. You have done that before. It is alright.

He felt the words settle into him in a way he could not fight.

Before.
A life where this had happened before.
A version of him that had lived moments he had no access to.

Mira's tone softened.

Can you meet me at the café on State Street? Same one as always.

He did not know the café.
He did not know where State Street was in this life.
He did not know what same one as always meant.

But he said, Yes. I will be there.

Mira sighed in relief.

Good. We need to talk today.

The call ended.

Kai lowered the phone slowly.
The world around him stayed steady, quiet, unchanged.
Yet the conversation pressed against him like truth he did not ask for.

He stood there for a moment, trying to understand the shape of the morning.

Something inside him whispered a thought he was not ready to admit.

This life already had a history.
He was simply arriving late to it.

Kai sat in the car a moment longer, letting the stillness settle around him. The call with Mira lingered like a sentence spoken in a language he almost understood. A quiet weight pressed against him, not heavy enough to frighten him but strong enough to make him feel unsteady inside his own life.

He started the engine.
The hum sounded familiar, but the way it vibrated through the seat felt slightly off.
A small reminder that even the ordinary had shifted its shape.

He pulled out of the driveway.
The neighborhood looked untouched, yet the details whispered something different.

A house with a blue door that had always been gray.
A tree taller than it should have been.
A street sign that felt newly placed.

Nothing dramatic.
Nothing disruptive.
Just the kind of differences that wait quietly for you
to notice them.

He approached the first stoplight.

The older man from earlier stood at the corner.
He should not have been able to reach this part of
the street so quickly, yet he stood there as if he had
always been meant to meet Kai here.

The man looked at him with calm, steady patience.

Be gentle with the morning.

He spoke as if the words held a meaning Kai had
not grown into yet.

Then he stepped off the curb and disappeared into
a narrow alley.

Kai watched the empty space where he vanished
and felt a faint pull in his chest, as if the world were
trying to draw him toward a truth he was not ready
to hold.

The light turned green.

He drove on.

The road curved into a part of town he recognized,
yet the recognition felt loose, like a memory seen
through soft glass.
Buildings stood where he expected them, but the

colors were wrong.
Shops he remembered had new names.
The small café on the corner had a different sign in the window.

He slowed the car and stared.

A chalkboard leaned against the door with neat handwriting.

Welcome back.

The words did not shock him.
They settled into him, calm and certain.
As if this life had been waiting for him to return to it.

He parked and stepped out.
For a moment, he stood at the threshold, feeling as if he were about to walk into a memory he had not earned.

The bell above the café door chimed as he entered.

The barista looked up with an easy smile.

The usual.

Kai froze.

The barista did not hesitate.
He reached for a cup with the familiarity of someone who had made it many times before.

I will have it ready in a minute, he said.

Kai looked around.
The tables were arranged in a way that felt practiced.
A plant near the window leaned toward the light in a familiar bend.
The air carried a scent that touched something inside him with the softness of a forgotten truth.

He sat near the back.

The barista placed a cup in front of him.
Black. No sugar.

The usual.

Kai stared at the drink.
He lifted it slowly and tasted it.

The flavor stirred something deep inside him.
Not memory.
Something quieter.
Recognition without origin.

A thought moved through him, soft and unsettling: this life knew him better than he knew himself.

He set the cup down and took a breath.

This was no longer a morning that felt off or borrowed.
This was a morning that belonged to a life that expected him to remember it.

A calm truth rose in him, steady and undeniable.

This was not the only version of the morning.
And this was not the only version of him.

For the first time, he wondered if he was remembering his life or if his life was remembering him.

For a moment, he felt the morning bend, quiet and slight, as if the world were preparing to move.

Something in him understood that the shift had only begun.

Chapter Three: The Rule of Elsewhere

Kai woke with the sense that the room had moved while he slept.

Not physically.
Not noisily.
Just shifted, the way a tide changes shape without announcing it.

He blinked and let the ceiling come into focus.
For a moment, it looked familiar.
He stared at it the way people stare at something they trust while waiting for the wrongness to surface.

Then it surfaced.

He could not remember falling asleep.

The light above him came from a window that should not have existed.
His bedroom did not have a window on that wall.

He sat up slowly.

The sheets were different.
A softer fabric.
A darker color.
The kind he once considered buying but never had a reason to.

He scanned the room.

New dresser.
New layout.
A plant in the corner, he had never owned.
A jacket draped neatly over a chair, a style he had never worn.

And on the nightstand sat a small silver key.

Thin.
Unmarked.
Light caught its surface in a way that made it look used, but not recently.
A key he had never seen, yet something about it felt faintly familiar, like an answer he had not asked for.

Nothing in the room belonged to the life he remembered.

He stood slowly.
The floor beneath him was hardwood instead of carpet.
His feet recognized none of the creaks.

He walked to the mirror on the closet door.

His reflection stared back.
Same face.
Same eyes.

But something subtle was different.

His hair was trimmed shorter.
His shoulders held a posture he had never
maintained for more than a day.
He looked like a version of himself who woke earlier,
moved with more discipline, and lived with less
hesitation.

He did not know that man.

For a moment, he felt like a guest inside his own
reflection, studying a life that had learned to move
without him.

A phone buzzed on the nightstand.

Not his phone.

Different case.
Different weight.
Different lock screen.

He picked it up.

A message glowed from a name he did not
recognize.
Not Mira.
Not anyone from the day before.

You left early again. Call me when you can.

Kai stared at the words.

Again.
A pattern he had not lived long enough to make.

He set the phone down and looked at the silver key.

The sight of it stirred something quiet inside him.
Recognition without memory.
A pull toward a life he had never entered, yet one
that seemed certain he belonged to it.

He felt the quiet loss of a life he had already left
behind.

He looked around the room once more.
Everything was steady.
Everything was in place.
Everything carried a history he had not lived.

He could feel the weight of choices he had never
made pressing gently against him, as if the room
remembered who he was supposed to be.

A patient truth settled in him with the slow clarity of
something that had waited its turn.

This was another life.
Another thread.
Another version of the morning.
And he had crossed into it without noise, without
warning, without permission.

His heart beat steadily, but something deeper inside
him shifted.
The world was no longer slipping.

It was choosing.

And it had chosen to move him again.

Kai took a breath.
The room waited in a calm that felt almost respectful, as if inviting him to understand the shape of his new reality.

He reached for the silver key.
It was warm, as if it had been held moments before he woke.

The world had changed for the second time.

Now he knew it would not be the last.

Chapter Four: The Life That Almost Fit

Kai stepped into the hallway with the silver key in his hand, the weight of it steady against his palm. The air felt different here. Cooler. Still. As if the walls had learned to hold their breath.

He walked slowly, letting the space tell him who he had become in this version of his life.

The hallway opened into a living room with tall windows.
A clean space.
Orderly.
Everything placed with intention.

On the coffee table sat a stack of books he did not recognize.
Titles about discipline.
Focus.
Structure.

He looked at them and felt a quiet distance inside himself, the way a person feels standing in a life they admire but never lived.

A faint thought brushed through him, the uneasy sense of stepping into a future someone else had chosen on his behalf.

A soft sound came from the kitchen.

He turned.

A woman stood at the counter.
Not Mira.
Someone else.

Her posture was relaxed, familiar, the posture of someone who had shared mornings with him for years. She looked over her shoulder and gave him a small smile.

You are up early, she said. Again.

Her voice held a calm certainty that settled into the room like a routine repeating itself.

Kai nodded slightly. Morning.

She poured hot water into a mug and slid it toward him without asking.
No sugar.
No cream.

The same way he drank it in the last life, yet the mug here was unchipped and perfectly smooth.

He took it.

The heat felt grounding in his hands, as if this version of him depended on simple routines to stay steady.

The woman leaned against the counter.

Rough night. You were restless again.

Again.

The word pressed against him with a quiet weight.

He took a sip and tasted a bitterness he had not expected.
Stronger.
Sharper.
More disciplined.

He set the mug down carefully.

I do not remember, he said.

She studied him for a moment. Not with suspicion. With familiarity.

You forget when you are stressed. You always have.

Her tone carried a softness shaped by years he had not lived with her.

She walked closer and brushed a hand across his shoulder.
A gentle, intimate gesture.
A gesture he did not know how to return.

I have to leave early today, she said. Your meeting is at nine. You should not be late again.

She kissed his cheek and grabbed her bag.

Call me when you get a moment.

Then she stepped out the door and disappeared down the stairs.

Kai stood in the quiet space she left behind.

He walked to the window.
Outside, the street looked different from both lives before it.
New neighborhood.
New light.
New rhythm.

He took another sip of the bitter coffee.

The flavor settled into him with an uneasy familiarity.
Not memory.
Not recognition.

Expectation.

This life had expectations of him.

He looked around the room slowly.

Everything here had a purpose.
Everything here belonged to a man with clearer habits and sharper boundaries.
A man who lived differently.
A man who woke earlier, worked harder, moved with intention.
A man he might have become.
He could feel a steadiness in this version of himself, a calm he had always wanted, yet something about

it unsettled him, as if the strength was borrowed and not truly his.

Kai felt something shift inside him.
A quiet tension.
A pull between who he was and who this life believed him to be.

He set the mug down.

The room stayed steady, but something in it waited for him to move in a way he did not understand yet.

He stepped forward, feeling the shape of this new life settle around him like a suit tailored for someone with his face, but not his history.

This life almost fit.
Almost.
But not quite.

He could feel the weight of a life lived through discipline instead of desire, and it unsettled him in a way the room did not hide.

For a moment, he felt himself reaching for a version of calm that did not belong to him, the kind of peace that asks for pieces of a person in return.

Kai dressed slowly, choosing clothes that seemed to belong to the man who lived here.
A pressed shirt.

Dark slacks.
Shoes that looked barely worn.

The outfit fit him well.
Almost too well.
As if it had been waiting for him.

He stepped into the hallway and noticed a small
desk near the door.
A leather-bound planner sat open, its pages filled
with tidy handwriting.
Meetings.
Calls.
Deadlines.
Plans arranged with deliberate precision.

He studied the list, searching for something familiar.
Nothing was.
Yet everything felt expected.

He closed the planner and slipped it into his bag.

Outside, the neighborhood moved with quiet
discipline.
Drives opening.
Engines starting.
Dogs walked on exact paths.
Even the light seemed to follow a practiced routine.

He walked toward an office building he sensed
belonged to him.
Inside, a receptionist looked up with relief.

Morning, Kai. You are early today.

Her voice carried routine the way some voices carry affection.

He nodded. Morning.

She handed him a folder.
You asked for this yesterday. You said the numbers mattered for the meeting.

He opened the folder.

Charts.
Projections.
Growth.
Success shaped into tidy graphs.

Everything belonged to a version of him who believed discipline could protect him from uncertainty.

He thanked her and stepped into his office.

The room was neat.
Quiet.
Organized with almost rigid intention.
A space designed to keep life under control.

A framed photo sat in the corner.
Him and the woman from the kitchen.
Smiling.
Sun behind them.
Her hand on his chest in a soft, familiar gesture.

But the eyes of the man in the picture told the real story.
Tired.
Watchful.
A hint of strain behind the smile.

A knock at the door broke the stillness.

A man entered.
Clean suit.
Confident posture.

Kai. Ready for it. You said the revisions were final.

The man spoke with the trust of someone who leaned on Kai's consistency.

Kai opened the folder again.
The numbers blurred.
Not because they were difficult.
Because they belonged to choices he had never made.

What did I tell you yesterday? His voice was steady but soft.

The man hesitated.

You said you were done second-guessing. You said you would stop changing course.

The sentence landed with a quiet weight.

Stop changing course.

A rule made by a version of himself he did not know.

Kai looked at the folder again.
This life was built on order.
Exactness.
A commitment to structure so tight there was no room for uncertainty.
Or honesty.
Or doubt.

A distraction disguised as discipline.

The man studied him.

Kai. You alright? This is not like you.

The same worry Mira had once carried.
The same pattern repeating itself.

Kai set the folder down gently.

I do not have the revisions.

The man paused.
Concern replaced confidence.
As if he had just glimpsed a crack in the foundation.

Kai felt something shift in the air.
A soft turn.
A quiet bending.
The same sensation that came before the last shift.

The man's voice reached him faintly.

Talk to me. You do not forget things.

Kai looked around the room.

The order.
The structure.
The discipline.
All of it shaped by a man who tried to outrun
uncertainty by controlling every corner of his life.

He felt the truth rise in him with steady clarity.

The calm in this life did not come from peace.
It came from control.
And control was only another way to stay distracted.

He suddenly understood that each perfect corner in
this room demanded a part of him he could not
afford to give.

He knew then that this life asked him to trade
himself for order, and he could not hold that
bargain.

The shift began.

Soft.
Unannounced.
Patient.

He closed his eyes.

This life almost fit.
Almost.
But not enough to hold him.

The world loosened its grip.

And the morning let him slip away.

Chapter Five: The Life He Once Wanted

Kai woke to the sound of silence that felt expensive.

The sheets beneath him were smooth, cool, and heavy. The kind of fabric people buy when they believe comfort can be purchased.
He opened his eyes slowly.

A ceiling stretched above him with clean lines and recessed lighting.
Soft, warm, intentional.
The kind of lighting that makes every room look like a photograph.

He pushed himself up.

The bed was large.
Too large.
Perfectly made except for the space he had disturbed.
Pillows arranged with the precision of someone who followed a ritual.

He stepped onto a polished hardwood floor.
No creaks.
No sound.
Only the steady whisper of quiet wealth.

He walked to the window.

The view opened across a city he did not recognize.
Tall buildings.
Glass towers catching morning light.
A skyline shaped by ambition.

Below, cars moved with intention.
People walked quickly.
Everything carried purpose.

He stood there for a moment, and let the life settle around him.

The apartment was modern.
Minimal.
Tasteful.
Not empty, but curated.
The kind of place someone builds after they have turned success into a habit.

A memory that did not belong to him stirred faintly.
Not a moment.
More a feeling.
The feeling of arriving somewhere he once believed mattered.

He walked toward the kitchen.

Marble counters.
Matte black fixtures.
A coffee machine sleek enough to look like a sculpture.

He pressed a button without knowing why.
Muscle memory.
Someone else's.

The machine hummed softly.
A clean sound.
A confident sound.

Steam rose.
The aroma filled the room with a richness that felt earned.

He took a cup and drank.

The flavor was bold and smooth.
Perfect.
The kind of coffee people brag about without realizing it reveals more about their pride than their taste.

He set the cup down and looked around again.

Everything was beautiful.
Everything was controlled.
Everything was the result of choices made with discipline.

This was a life someone would fight to keep.

A door opened behind him.

Kai.

A woman stepped into the kitchen.
Tall.

Graceful.
Calm.
Her presence carried the quiet confidence of someone who had learned to navigate polished spaces.

Her voice held no surprise.
Only familiarity.

You are up early. I thought you would sleep in after last night.

Kai nodded slightly, unsure how to answer.

She walked closer and touched his arm gently.

You worked late. You always do. I told you to rest more.

She kissed his cheek and moved to the counter, opening a neatly organized drawer.

Every utensil aligned.
Every tool in its place.
A world built on accuracy.

She turned back to him with a soft smile.

You have a meeting at the tower today. They want your final approval. You seemed excited about it yesterday.

Kai held her gaze.

What did I say yesterday?

She paused, studying him.

You said this deal was the one you had been waiting for. The one that finally makes all of this feel worth it.

Her hand lifted slightly, motioning to the apartment.
To the life.
To everything shining quietly around him.

Kai looked around again, slower this time.

The beauty.
The order.
The view.
The success.

He felt something move inside him.
A small shift.
A quiet tension.

Not fear.
Not confusion.

Distance.

A distance between the man who built this life and the man standing in it.

She stepped closer.

Are you alright? You are quiet this morning.

He nodded again, even though he did not feel the nod.

I am fine, he said softly.

She believed him without question.

Good. They are expecting you. Do not be late. This is important.

She walked toward the bedroom, leaving him alone in the kitchen filled with quiet perfection.

Kai looked out at the skyline again.

A city built on ambition.
A view built on hard work.
A life built on arrival.
Yet something about it felt hollow.
A life could shine and still leave a shadow inside the person living it.
Not broken.
Not wrong.
Just empty in a way beauty could not hide.

He could feel that this life was held together by achievement, and achievement had a way of keeping a person busy enough to forget what they had lost.

He took another sip of coffee.

The flavor was perfect, but it did not reach him.

He stood there, steady in the morning light, and felt a truth forming in the quiet space between breaths.

This was the life he once believed he wanted.

But now he could feel the cost.

And the cost was waiting for him.

Kai arrived at the tower just before midmorning.
The building rose above the city with the calm
confidence of something built to last.
Glass.
Steel.
Edges clean enough to make the sky look
intentional.

He stepped through the doors.

The lobby opened around him like a polished
cathedral.
Quiet marble.
Soft echoes.
People moving with a purpose he felt but did not
share.

A security guard nodded at him.

Morning, Mr. Hale.

The name settled into the space between them.

Hale.

The version of him who built this life had taken a
different last name.
Or maybe this world had given it to him.

Kai nodded back, unsure whether to accept it or question it.

He stepped into the elevator.
The doors closed.
The ride was smooth enough that it felt like floating.

On the thirty-second floor, a receptionist greeted him with a smile that did not belong to a stranger.

There you are. They are waiting for you in the conference room. You said you wanted a moment to gather yourself first.

Kai nodded as if the memory might return if he played along.

He walked toward a glass-walled room at the end of the hall.
He paused outside, letting his eyes take in the place.

Long table.
Tall windows.
Chairs angled with precision.

A space meant for people who believed their decisions could move the world.

He entered.

Conversations quieted.
Heads turned.
Smiles lifted.

There he is.

Kai took a seat near the head of the table.
The chair felt molded to a version of him he had not yet met.

A man across from him leaned forward.

You ready to finish this? You said you were done compromising.

Kai opened the folder in front of him.
Charts.
Documents.
A proposal shaped by ambition.

He scanned the numbers.
Something familiar about the structure.
Something unfamiliar about the intent.

He looked up.

What is the purpose of this again?

The room stilled for a slight moment.

The man frowned gently.

Kai, this is your plan. Your vision. You said it would redefine the market.

Another person spoke.

You pushed hard for this. You said it was time to claim what was yours.

Kai studied their faces.
The admiration in their eyes.
The expectation.
The way they looked at him as if he carried the
blueprint for all of them.

A strange feeling rose in him.

Not pride.
Not fear.
Something quieter.

Separation.

They admired a version of him he did not trust.
A version built on demonstration instead of truth.

He looked back at the documents.
Each page was precise.
Each line calculated.
Each projection designed to prove something.

It became clear.
This life was not driven by meaning.
It was driven by momentum.
A polished momentum that never allowed a person
to stop long enough to ask why.

He set the papers down.

A voice spoke beside him.

You alright. You usually come in with that focus of
yours.

That focus.

Another expectation tied to a person he was not.

Kai leaned back slightly and let the room settle around him.

The walls were glass, yet the space felt closed.
Contained.
Shaped by ambition so tight it left no room for anything else.

He looked out at the skyline.
Tall buildings.
Sharp shadows.
A city moving without him.

He felt a quiet truth surface inside him.

Success was the reflection.
Not the substance.

The man across from him tapped the folder.

Well. What do you think?

Kai answered slowly.

I am thinking.

A soft wave of concern moved across the table.

Someone else spoke, gentler this time.

Kai, if you are tired, we can reschedule. You looked exhausted yesterday. You said you needed this win to feel whole again.

The words made something tighten in him.

Feel whole again.

He did not remember ever saying that.
But somewhere deeper, he knew the type of man who would.

A man who believed wholeness came from winning.

He took a breath.

A memory flickered.
Not a scene.
Only a feeling.

A version of him in this life, standing at this table, fighting for recognition he had already earned.

A man chasing validation he did not need.

He closed the folder.

The room waited, patient and tense.

He looked at each face.
People who respected him.
People who depended on him.
People who saw him as someone he was not sure he had ever aspired to be.

They looked at him and saw a leader.
He looked at them and saw a mirror.

A mirror of a life shaped by achievement instead of alignment.

He exhaled slowly.

This life did not feel wrong.
It simply did not feel like him.

The meeting paused again as if the room sensed something shifting.

He heard someone whisper.

He does not look like himself today.

Kai held the folder loosely in his hand.

The truth rose in him, steady and undeniable.

This was the life he once wanted.

But it was not the life he was made for.

He could feel that success had sharpened him, but it had also hollowed something important inside him.

He felt the first quiet bend of the air.
A soft pressure.
A gentle tilt.
The world preparing to move.

The shift had not arrived yet.
But he could feel it gathering.
Waiting for the moment the truth became too clear to ignore.

He closed his eyes for a breath.

Then he opened them.

The room was the same.

Which meant everything was already beginning to change.

Kai left the conference room and stepped into the hallway.
The air felt thinner here.
Still bright.
Still polished.
But thinner, as if the building itself had become aware of him in a new way.

He walked toward the elevators, the soft echo of his footsteps following him down the corridor.

As he passed a glass office, he caught his reflection in the window.
Sharp suit.
Steady posture.
The image of someone who knew exactly who he was.

Except the eyes.

There was a tiredness there.
A quiet ache beneath the surface.
A hollow he could not ignore.

He kept walking.

The elevator doors opened.
He stepped inside and pressed the button for the lobby.

A man slipped in before the doors closed. A colleague.
You good? Kai. You seemed off in there.

Kai nodded. Yes.

But the man studied him with the uneasy familiarity of someone who had seen this version of him unravel before.

You know, he said quietly, yesterday you told me something. You said that if this deal did not fix the way you felt inside, nothing would.

Kai looked at him.

The man shrugged.

I thought you were joking. But you did not look like someone who was joking.

The elevator chimed.
The doors opened.

The man walked out, leaving the words hanging in the small metal room.

Fix the way you felt inside.

Kai stepped into the lobby.

The space was elegant.
Calm.
Designed to make success feel inevitable.

He walked through the rotating doors and into the city sunlight.

The street buzzed around him.
People in suits moved quickly.
Cars streamed by in steady rhythm.

Life here was focused.
Determined.
Ambitious.

He walked down the sidewalk, letting the city shape itself around him.

As he approached a crosswalk, he heard two voices behind him.

You think he is alright?

I do not know. He looked lost today.

Lost.

The word pressed against him, soft and undeniable.

He crossed the street and entered a small courtyard
beside the tower.
A quiet space.
Trees standing in order.
Benches placed with intention.

He sat on one and let the morning settle.

A digital billboard rose above the courtyard.
A bright, polished advertisement filled the screen.
A photo of him.

Smiling.
Confident.
Standing in front of the tower, he had just left.

The text beneath the image read:

A Vision Built on Certainty.

Kai stared at the picture.

His own smile looked like something practiced.
Just enough teeth.
Just enough warmth.
Just enough performance to pass as authenticity.

He watched the image fade into another ad.

A product launch.
A luxury development.
Another face.
Another smile.

The billboard cycled back to him again.

He watched the same smile he had studied once before.
It struck him then that success had not sharpened him. It had thinned him.
The same polished version of himself.
A version trained to inspire trust.

Except he felt none of the trust now.
Not in the smile.
Not in the man behind it.
Not in the life that demanded it.

A small truth rose in him, soft and steady.

He had built this life to be seen.

Not to be known.

He realized that success could fill a life with motion, but it could not give it direction.

He took a slow breath.

The air around him shifted.
Almost imperceptible.
Almost polite.

A leaf on the nearest tree trembled, though the wind was still.

A faint pressure pressed against the space around him.
Not heavy.
Not sudden.

Just certain.

The first quiet sign that the world was preparing to release him.

He closed his eyes.

A distant hum grew louder, not from the street, but from somewhere deeper.
A hum that felt like a thread pulling loose.

He opened his eyes.

The courtyard looked the same.
The tower stood tall.
The billboard cycled through its bright reels.

But something inside him had already stepped away.

Success had brought him here.
But it could not keep him.

He felt the distance between the man he became and the man he meant to be widen with quiet certainty.

The shift began before he could name it.

The world tilted softly.
The light bent in a way the eye could barely catch.
The air thickened, then thinned.

He exhaled, slow and steady.

The city continued around him as if nothing had changed.

But everything had.

The morning loosened its hold.

And he felt himself slip into whatever waited next.

Chapter Six: The Life He Tried to Fix

Kai woke to a room that felt heavy before he even opened his eyes.

Not dark.
Not cold.
Just heavy.
The kind of heaviness that settles in places where someone has been trying too long.

He opened his eyes slowly.

The ceiling above him was plain.
Off-white.
A faint water stain near the corner, shaped like something that had once been repaired but never truly solved.

He pushed himself up in bed.

The sheets were tangled, not from restlessness, but from two people trying to sleep through a tension neither of them had the energy to name.

He looked to his right.

The other side of the bed was empty, but the pillow carried the shape of someone who had risen early and quietly.

A soft sound came from the kitchen.

Kai stood and walked through the small hallway.

Family photos lined the walls.
Not glamorous ones.
Honest ones.

A tired smile.
A forced pose.
A moment captured to convince themselves that
everything was alright.

He stopped in front of one picture.

Him and a woman.
Her hand on his chest.
A smile that almost reached her eyes.
Almost.

He felt something press against him from inside.
Recognition wrapped in sadness.

Someone had loved him here.
Someone still did.
But the warmth in the photo was holding on to
something that needed more than love to survive.

He stepped into the kitchen.

She stood at the counter.
Same height as the woman in the successful life.
Different posture.
Shoulders slightly hunched.
Hair pulled back in a way that said she had a long
morning ahead.

She turned, surprised to see him.

You are awake early.

Her voice was soft, worn, the kind of voice people develop after years of trying to make things work.

Kai nodded. Morning.

She poured coffee into a mug and slid it toward him.

I fixed the machine. It kept leaking again. I thought you were going to take a look at it last night.

There was no accusation in her tone.
Only expectation.
The kind that builds slowly, the kind that grows from carrying responsibilities alone.

Kai looked at the machine.
A small flicker of memory surfaced.
Not a full scene.
Just a feeling.

He had promised something in this life.
Promised many things.
Things he had never actually done.

She poured herself a cup and sat across from him.

You have a meeting later. Daniel called twice. He needs you to talk to the landlord again. And your sister texted. She said she cannot figure out the insurance paperwork without you.

Kai listened.
The list grew.
Names.
Needs.
Weights.

She took a breath.

I know it is a lot.
But you always handle it.

Her eyes held something he understood instantly.

Dependence.
Hope.
Fear.
A belief in him that had cost her too much.

He sat down.

The chair creaked beneath him.
A small sound that hinted at years of use.
Years of repairs done halfway.
Years of trying to keep things together.

She reached across the table and touched his hand.

I know you are tired.
But we are close. You said that last week. If we can
just get through this month, things will settle.

Her voice cracked slightly at the edge of the
sentence.

Not from weakness.
From carrying too much for too long.

Kai looked at her hand on his.
Warm.
Gentle.
Familiar in a way that hurt.

This was not a life built on excitement.
Not a life built on ambition.
Not a life built on discipline.

This was a life built on repair.

Every corner.
Every gesture.
Every room carried the quiet strain of things held together by effort instead of ease.

A thought rose in him with slow clarity.

He had become the fix in this life.
Not the partner.
Not the man.
Not the self.
The fix.

He heard a thud in the other room.
A drawer stuck.
A hinge squeaking.

Another reminder of something that needed attention.

He looked at the woman across from him.

Her eyes were tired, but hopeful.
Hopeful in a way that pulled something heavy from inside him.

She waited for him to speak.
To promise.
To repair.
To be the answer again.

He could feel that this life was held together by his effort, and effort had quietly replaced who he was becoming.

Kai breathed in slowly.

This was not the life he had once wanted.
This was the life he had tried to keep from falling apart.

The life he kept trying to fix.

Kai stepped outside into a gray morning.
The sky looked undecided, holding its color the way a person holds a thought they are not ready to say.
The air felt thick, not with weather, but with expectation.

His phone buzzed.

First message.
Daniel: *Call me. The landlord is threatening to raise the rent again.*

Second message.
His sister: *I sent the forms. Please look before noon. I cannot afford another mistake.*

Third message.
Unknown number.
A voicemail from someone he sensed he should know.

He slid the phone into his pocket.

The weight of it felt heavier than the device itself.

He walked toward his car.
The hood had a dent on one side, evidence of something repaired halfway.
The left mirror was taped carefully.
The inside smelled faintly of old coffee and tired mornings.

He started the engine.
It coughed once, then settled into a soft rattle.

Another reminder of something that needed attention.

He drove through the neighborhood.
Houses lined the street in muted colors.
A lawn unmowed.

A fence leaning.
Small signs of lives held together by effort.

At a stop sign, an older neighbor waved him over.

Kai rolled down the window.

I hate to bother you, the man said, but you still have that toolbox. My sink is leaking again. I would fix it myself, but you know how these hands get.

He lifted a trembling hand as proof.

Kai nodded. I can stop by later.

The neighbor smiled with quiet relief.

You always take care of us. Thank you.

Kai watched him walk away, shoulders slumped in a familiar tiredness.

Another buzz from his phone.

Daniel again. *Please, man. I am sinking over here. You are the only one who listens.*

He drove on.

The light changed.
Cars moved.
The world continued.

But inside the car, something tightened.

The sense that he was moving through a life where everyone reached for him because they believed he could carry what they could not.

He wondered how many lives he had lived where everyone reached for him like this.

He turned onto a narrow street and pulled into the parking lot of a small community center.

Inside, a staff member greeted him with a hopeful smile.

Kai. Perfect timing. The printer jammed again. And the volunteers keep asking when you can train them on the new system.

Her voice held a familiar warmth.
Trust wrapped in need.

He followed her into an office.

Papers stacked in uneven piles.
Half-filled forms.
A computer with a cracked screen.
A bulletin board filled with reminders written in multiple handwriting styles.

He opened the printer and worked quietly.

As he fixed it, she spoke.

I do not know how you keep all of this together.
You have your partner.
Your family.

Your brother's situation.
This place.
Your job.
Everything.
You never fall apart.

Kai paused.

The comment was meant as praise.
But it pressed into him like a truth spoken too
casually.

Never fall apart.

He tightened a screw and closed the printer tray.

The machine whirred to life.

The staff member exhaled in relief.

See. This is why we count on you.

Kai stepped back and watched the paper feed
through the machine.

A clean sheet.
Then another.
Then another.

Perfect.
Smooth.
Efficient.

He felt none of the satisfaction the moment
expected.

His phone buzzed again.

His partner.
Her message read: *Can you pick up the groceries.
And maybe talk to my brother. He said he needs
help. I am sorry. I know it is a lot.*

Kai closed his eyes.

A soft ache rose in him.
Not pain.
Not fear.

A kind of quiet exhaustion that felt older than this
life.

He looked around the room.

The jammed printer.
The cracked screen.
The taped mirror on his car.
The leaking machine in the kitchen.
The list of people who needed him.
The hope in their voices.

This life was not built on chaos.
It was built on dependency.

A world he held together with effort.
Effort that had become the cost of staying needed.

He walked back to his car.

The sky had darkened slightly, as if reflecting
something inside him.

He sat behind the wheel.

The engine hummed under his hand.
Soft.
Strained.

He could feel the day waiting for him.

Waiting for the next problem.
Waiting for the next fix.
Waiting for him to hold together what no one else could.

A truth rose inside him.

This life did not ask him to be whole.
It asked him to be useful.

He could feel parts of himself slipping into the spaces he was trying to hold for everyone else.

He placed his hands on the steering wheel and let that truth settle.

It landed like something he had been trying not to hear.

Something that had always been there.

Kai walked back toward the house with the slow, weighted steps of someone returning to a place he was not sure he belonged. The quiet followed him closely. It felt tighter now, as if the air had learned the shape of his hesitation.

Inside, the rooms waited in a calm that did not comfort him. Everything was still in place. Everything was orderly. Everything was arranged to make him feel accomplished.

He set his keys on the counter and listened to the soft clink echo through the kitchen.
A sound that should have felt familiar.
A sound that felt borrowed instead.

He walked toward the hallway mirror and stopped in front of it. The reflection staring back looked steady. Focused. Collected. The kind of man who never missed a deadline and never let his guard slip.

But the eyes told the truth.

A tiredness lived there.
A tiredness that did not belong to the life he remembered.
A tiredness that came from carrying a version of himself that was built for function, not for becoming.

He pressed a palm against the cool surface of the glass.

Something is missing.
The thought rose inside him without permission.

Not from this house.
Not from this job.
Not from this version of success.

From him.

He turned slightly and looked at the living room.
Everything was arranged perfectly. The kind of
perfection that asked a person to maintain it at all
costs. The kind that required constant tending.
Constant effort. Constant control.

A perfection that did not leave much space for
truth.

He closed his eyes and felt the stillness settle on his
skin.
A stillness too smooth to be real.

In the silence, something shifted.

Not in the room.
In him.

A faint pull inside his chest.
Soft.
Steady.
Certain.

He had felt it before, in other lives, at the edge of
other mornings.

A warning.
A signal.
The quiet tilt of the world preparing to move.

He opened his eyes.

The room looked the same.
The light had not changed.
The air had not moved.

But the truth had arrived.

This life carried him with discipline.
But it did not carry him with meaning.

He felt the quiet truth settle in him. He had built a life that demanded everything but never returned what mattered.

He felt the weight of every life pressing through the cracks of this one, each version of him asking the same unspoken question: how long can you hold together what is already breaking.

He stepped back from the mirror.
The air thinned.
The pull deepened.

The shift was coming.

Slow.
Patient.
Certain.

He stood in the center of the room, letting the moment settle around him like the breath before a question.

Then the world softened.
Edges blurred.
Light bent.

And Kai felt the life slip from his hands, gentle as a tired truth finally letting go.

Kai woke to warmth.

Not light.
Not sound.
Warmth.

A quiet, steady warmth pressed against his back, the kind that only comes from another body, breath moving in a calm rhythm he felt before he heard it.

He kept his eyes closed for a moment.

Not out of fear.
Not out of confusion.
Out of something softer.

A part of him did not want to disturb whatever this was.

A hand rested lightly on his shoulder.
Familiar.

Unforced.
A touch that carried history.

He opened his eyes slowly.

The room was dim, lit only by a soft line of morning filtering through curtains he had never seen. The air carried the faint scent of lavender. A blanket he did not recognize lay tangled around him.

He turned.

She slept facing him.

A woman with gentle features, hair falling loosely across her cheek, her breathing steady in the quiet space between them. Her face was peaceful in the way people look when they trust the room, the morning, and the person beside them.

He watched her for a moment.

Something inside him pulled tight, then loosened.

Recognition.
Not memory.
Recognition.

As if she belonged to a part of him he had not met yet, but always suspected existed.

She stirred.

Her eyes opened with the slow, unhurried clarity of someone waking into a life that already felt right.

Morning, she whispered.

The softness in her voice told him everything.

She loved him here.

Deeply.
Quietly.
Without hesitation.

He swallowed, unable to trust his own voice yet.

She brushed her fingers against his jaw, tracing him the way people do when they know a face by heart.

You went to bed early. You were tired, she said.

Her tone held no worry.
No suspicion.
Only care shaped by years he had not lived.

He searched her eyes, trying to find the hint of a memory he could claim.

Nothing came.

Only warmth.

She sat up slightly, leaning on her elbow, studying him.

You look different, she said softly. Not bad. Just distant.

He forced a small smile. I am alright.

She nodded, accepting it without needing more.

That was the danger.

She trusted him here.

She trusted who he was in this life.

She kissed his forehead, slow and gentle.

For a moment, he felt something dangerous inside him soften, a quiet part of himself leaning toward her in a way that frightened him.

Come downstairs when you are ready. I made breakfast.

She slipped out of bed and moved with the ease of someone used to sharing space with him, her silhouette familiar in a way that pressed on him quietly.

Kai sat up.

The bed felt too soft.
The room felt too warm.
His chest felt too full.

He looked at the pillow she left behind, the faint imprint of her head still there.

Something inside him shook.

He had forgotten what it felt like for a morning to greet him instead of need him.

A version of his life where he was loved this deeply was not a blessing.
It was a risk.

Because part of him already wanted to stay.

He closed his eyes.

This life did not distract him with comfort, control, or achievement.

It distracted him with belonging.

And belonging was the one thing he had never learned to walk away from.

Kai stepped downstairs, each step slow and steady, the air carrying a warmth that felt like a memory he had not lived. Something about this house held the shape of him. Not the him he knew, but the him he could have been.

The kitchen light was on.

Soft.
Golden.
Inviting.

She stood at the stove, humming quietly, the kind of unconscious melody people make when they feel safe. The pan sizzled gently. Steam curled into the air in a calm spiral.

She turned when she sensed him behind her.

There you are.
Her smile was small and real. Not performed. Not polite.
A smile shaped by mornings shared.

He felt it in his chest, subtle and unwelcome in its power.

Sit. Breakfast is almost ready.

He sat at the small wooden table.
Two mugs sat waiting.
One black.
One with cinnamon.
She slid the cinnamon mug toward him without asking.

His breath caught.

He had never told her he preferred cinnamon in anything.

But here, she already knew.

She poured his drink with the gentle, practiced motion of someone who knew the weight of the cup, the speed of the pour, the exact level he liked.

He watched her move around the kitchen.

Nothing about her felt unfamiliar.
Everything about her felt known.
And that was the part that shook him.

She sat across from him, resting her chin in her hand.

You have that look again.

What look?

The one you get when you are in your head before the day even starts.

Her voice carried understanding. Not judgment.
A kind of closeness that made the room feel smaller in a comforting way.

He tried to speak, but the words stayed behind his breath.

She reached across the table and took his hand.
Not for reassurance.
Not out of worry.

Out of habit.

Her thumb brushed the back of his hand in slow circles, a gesture he recognized in his body but not in his memory.

She said something in a whisper only someone who had seen him at his lowest would know:

You have survived worse mornings than this.

You know you do not have to carry everything alone, she said softly.

He felt the truth of her belief.
He felt how deeply she meant it.
He felt the weight of a life where someone loved him without needing him to earn it.

It terrified him.

He looked at her hand in his and felt something shift.

Not the world.
Not the morning.

Him.

A quiet part of him leaned toward her.
A part of him that had been untouched in every other life.

She squeezed his hand gently.

Stay with me today, she said.
We have been missing each other lately.

He swallowed hard.

This life was not asking him to be useful.
Not asking him to be strong.
Not asking him to perform.

It was asking him to belong.

And belonging was the most dangerous distraction of all.

Kai stepped outside with her after breakfast, the morning air soft against his skin. The street felt familiar in a way he could not explain, as if he had walked it a thousand times in another version of himself.

She locked the door and slid her hand into his with a quiet ease. No hesitation. No pause. Her fingers intertwined with his as if the gesture lived in the bones of this life.

They walked down the steps together.

A neighbor across the street waved.

Morning, Kai. Morning, Lily.

Lily.
Her name shaped itself inside him as if it had always been there, tucked behind something quiet and waiting. He glanced at her. She smiled at the neighbor and then at him, the kind of smile that carried years of shared mornings.

He felt a pull in his chest, soft and steady.

They continued down the block.

Children on bikes sped past them. A woman tending to her garden greeted him with a warmth that felt practiced. A man jogging slowed just enough to clap Kai on the shoulder.

See you tonight. Do not forget.

Kai nodded on instinct, though he had no idea what tonight was.

Lily noticed and squeezed his hand gently.

The dinner party, she said. You promised you would not disappear early this time.

He breathed in.
Her words were not sharp.
They carried affection more than expectation.

They turned the corner.

A small café came into view. The sign above the door was hand-painted. The windows were fogged with warmth. The place looked like the kind of spot people returned to without thinking.

As they approached, the barista inside looked up and grinned.

There he is. I saved your table.

Their table.

Kai felt something shift inside him again.

They stepped inside, and Lily greeted people by name. Everyone responded with familiarity, their eyes moving to Kai with ease, as if he were an expected part of the room.

A woman from across the café waved.

Kai, Lily said you finally finished that project. You must feel lighter.

He forced a small smile. Something like that.

The woman nodded approvingly, returning to her drink.

Kai sat at the table the barista had saved. Lily sat across from him, resting her elbows on the wood.

You always look overwhelmed the first few moments when we walk in here, she said gently.

Do I?

Every time. Then you settle in. Everyone cares about you here. You know that.

He looked around the room.

People laughed easily.
Voices blended softly.
The atmosphere felt warm enough to rest in.

He felt another pull.
Stronger this time.
A quiet invitation to stay.

Lily reached across the table again, brushing the back of his hand with her fingers.

You do not have to leave right after coffee today.
Stay a little longer with me.

He reached for a memory of Mira, and the name felt
thin, as if distance had begun to erase it.

His breath caught.
The softness in her voice made something inside
him loosen and tighten at the same time.

He looked around again.

The world in this life did not need him to be strong.
It did not need him to fix anything.
It only needed him to be present.

This was the life that wanted him.
This was the life that believed in him.
This was the life that loved him.

And for the first time, Kai felt something dangerous
settle inside him.

A part of him wondered what it would cost to stay.

The dinner party was warm.

Soft lights.
Low laughter.
The scent of food drifting through a house that felt
lived in and loved.

Kai moved through the rooms beside Lily, watching the way people greeted her. They hugged her with real affection, speaking to her with the easy rhythm of long friendship. She introduced him each time, her hand resting on his back with gentle pride.

Everyone knew him here.
Everyone trusted him.
Everyone believed in the version of him that lived in this life.

He felt the weight of that belief settle onto his shoulders.

Lily guided him to the table.
Her hand lingered on his.
Her smile held something soft and certain.

You have been distant lately, she said quietly, just loud enough for him to hear. I want you with me tonight. Present.

He nodded because she deserved that.
He nodded because this life deserved that.
And for a brief moment, he felt himself meaning it.

Dinner began.

Voices rose in easy conversation.
Stories.
Jokes.
Shared history.

Kai listened.

There was a rhythm to the room, a rhythm he almost fell into. People laughed at things he did not understand. They referenced moments he had not lived. Yet each time, Lily brushed her hand against his arm, grounding him, filling the gaps, making the unfamiliar feel less strange.

He felt himself almost relax.

Almost.

Then someone raised a glass.

To Kai, one of the best people I know.

Everyone lifted their glasses.
Eyes warm.
Faces open.
Belief shining toward him.

And Kai felt something inside him crack.

The man they toasted was not him.
Not the him who stood here.
Not the him who had slipped through realities.
Not the him who woke each day unsure of where he belonged.

They were celebrating a version of him he had never met.

Lily looked at him with pride that made his chest ache.

She reached for his hand under the table.

He reached back.

For a moment, the world steadied.

For a moment, he wished the world would stop shifting. Just once. Just here.

Then it slipped.

A soft bending of light.
A quiet distortion.
A gentle pull behind his ribs.

He tried to ignore it.
Tried to stay inside the warmth of the room.
Tried to hold the life that held him so carefully.

But the shift grew stronger.

Lily noticed.

Kai.
Her voice trembled.
Talk to me.

He looked at her, at the fear rising in her eyes, and wanted more than anything to give her something true.

But truth would hurt her.
And lies would hurt him.
And silence was the only language he had left.

The pull deepened.

He felt the Mira memory thinning again.
He felt the kitchen from another life blur.
He felt the man at the café fade.
He felt Lily's fingers tightening around his.

Do not drift, she whispered. Stay with me.

He tried.

He truly tried.

But the world was already loosening its hold.

Faces blurred at the edges.
Voices softened.
The warmth of Lily's hand became a fading
brightness.

Her voice broke.

Please. Do not leave me like this.

He wanted to stay.
He wanted to choose this table.
This laughter.
This softness.
This woman who loved him across a life he did not
earn.

But wanting was not enough.

The shift took him gently.
Almost apologetically.

The last thing he saw was Lily reaching for him.

The last thing he felt was her hand slipping through his.

Then the world folded, and the life that had loved him could not hold him any longer.

Chapter Seven: The Life Without Edges

Kai woke into quiet.

Not the kind that comforts.
Not the kind that warns.
A neutral quiet.
A quiet that asked nothing of him.

He opened his eyes slowly.
The ceiling above him was smooth and unmarked.
Perfect white.
Perfect stillness.
A surface that had never held a story.

He sat up.

The bed was neatly made except for the space his
body had shaped.
No other warmth.
No other imprint.
Just one life pressing softly into the sheets and
rising again without consequence.

He looked around the room.

Everything was arranged with clean intention.
Muted colors.
Soft lines.
No clutter.
No chaos.

Nothing broken.
Nothing precious.

It was the kind of room someone might choose if they wanted their life to feel manageable.

A faint calm settled over him.
Not comfort.
Not peace.
Just a soft absence where feelings might have lived.

He stepped into the hallway.
The air moved in a slow, predictable rhythm, as if the house exhaled on schedule.
The walls were bare except for one framed print.
A horizon line.
Perfectly straight.
Perfectly centered.
So balanced it felt almost unnatural.

Something in him tightened for a moment.
A small flicker.
A brief signal that the room wanted to teach him something he was not ready to hear.

He walked into the kitchen.

The appliances gleamed.
The counters were spotless.
A fruit bowl held three identical apples, each one polished as if they had been arranged for display more than for eating.

He picked one up and set it back down.
The bowl did not shift.
Nothing here shifted unless someone intended it to.

He made coffee without thinking.
One scoop.
Water.
Button.

The machine hummed its soft, perfect hum.
A sound without personality.
A sound engineered to never interrupt.

He poured the coffee into a plain white mug.
He lifted it.
He drank.

The taste was fine.
Not good.
Not bad.
Just fine.

He felt the neutrality of it move through him.

For a moment, something inside him pushed
against the stillness.
A faint irritation.
A question without words.
A reminder that even numbness has edges.

But the feeling faded quickly, swallowed by the
quiet shape of the room.

He walked to the window.
Pulled back the curtain.
Outside, the neighborhood was washed in soft
morning light.
Lawns trimmed.
Cars clean.
No noise.
No rush.
No urgency.
The world sat evenly, like a lake without wind.

A man across the street walked his dog.
The dog trotted at a steady pace.
Never pulling.
Never lagging.
The leash was slack, as if both of them had agreed
to remove struggle from their lives.

Kai watched them pass.

They did not look up.
They did not wave.
Not out of rudeness.
Out of rhythm.

Everyone here moved in rhythms that protected
them from wanting too much.

He breathed in.
The air felt precise.
Measured.
Like a room that had learned how to regulate itself.

As he stood there, a thought came to him, not loud, not sharp, just a quiet truth rising from a place that still remembered how to speak.

Perhaps a life does not need to break to become dangerous.
Perhaps it can simply fail to move.

He let the curtain fall back into place.

The house waited for him.
Patient.
Unchanging.
Ready to offer him another day that asked nothing and gave nothing.

A day that could repeat forever.

He felt the faintest pull inside his chest.
The smallest reminder of who he had been in other mornings.
It flickered once, then dimmed.

Still, the truth it carried did not vanish.

A life without pain, without chaos, without need, could still take everything from a person.

It could take them slowly.

Quietly.

By giving them nothing to push against.

Kai stood in the center of the room, surrounded by the soft balance of a world designed to keep him steady.

A world that would let him drift until he no longer noticed he was drifting.

He closed his eyes.

The stillness pressed in.

And for the first time in this life, he felt the loneliness inside the calm.

Kai stepped outside.

The morning air met him with the same steady temperature it always seemed to hold, neither warm nor cold, as if the weather had agreed not to interrupt anyone's plans. The sidewalk was clean. The sky a pale, even blue. Nothing in the world reached toward him or demanded anything from him.

He walked without hurry.

Not because he felt calm.
Because there was nothing to hurry for.

Cars passed in smooth, spaced timing, each one identical in its patience. No horns. No rush. No sudden movements. A world that behaved exactly as it should.

He crossed the street.

A woman jogging approached from the opposite direction. Her pace was perfect, rhythmic, unwavering. When she passed him, she nodded once, friendly but not curious. It was the kind of acknowledgment that expected nothing in return.

He nodded back.

The moment ended the instant it began.

He continued down the block, noticing the way each house sat evenly spaced, each lawn the same length, each window reflecting the same unbothered light. It felt less like a neighborhood and more like a row of choices someone had arranged for people who no longer questioned their lives.

His phone buzzed.

A calendar reminder.

No urgent tone.
No message from anyone.
Just a notification for a meeting that required nothing from him but presence.

He dismissed it.

The action gave him no relief, no guilt, no shift in his pulse.

Just an empty checkbox in a day that would offer many more.

He passed a small shop, a bakery.
Inside, people stood in line, speaking in soft voices, none of them interrupting the air. Their movements were gentle, predictable, as if everyone understood the unspoken rule of this life:

Do not disturb the balance.

He kept walking.

Halfway down the next street, he paused.

It was not a memory that stopped him.
Not fear.
Not recognition.

Just a sensation.

As if something in him expected a tug, a pull from another life, another version of himself, another morning.

Nothing came.

He waited anyway.

A brief stillness spread through him, the kind that felt less like peace and more like being left out of his own life.

For a moment, he wondered if he was the one standing still or if the day had simply learned how to move without him.

Still nothing.

He continued walking.

The absence disturbed him more than any presence would have.

A bird landed on a fence nearby. It chirped once, a single sound, then fell silent. A moment later, another bird landed beside it. Both sat still, facing the same direction, not moving until they lifted off at the same time, wings catching air in perfect synchronicity.

Kai felt something in his chest tighten again.

Too perfect.
Too even.
Too quiet.

He approached a small pond at the end of the street. The water was still, glass-like, reflecting the sky with unnerving precision. Not a ripple. Not a breeze. As if the world had agreed to remain undisturbed for his arrival.

He stared at the surface.

His reflection looked back at him.
Same face.
Same eyes.

But the stillness around him made the reflection feel wrong, as if the world was holding his image in place rather than allowing it to exist.

He crouched slightly and dipped two fingers into the water.

A ripple formed.

Slow at first, then wider.

He watched the pattern shift the reflection, delicate, temporary, alive.

For a moment, he felt something loosen inside him.
A tiny lift.
A reminder that he could still disturb the world if he wanted to.

But the water settled again.
Quickly.
Perfectly.

As if nothing had ever touched it.

Kai stood.

He should have felt calm.
Instead, he felt something he could not yet name.

Not sadness.
Not fear.
Not loneliness.

A thinning.

As if he were becoming less visible to himself.

He turned away from the pond and walked back toward the street. The houses waited. The air waited. The world waited.

For the first time in this life, the waiting felt less like patience and more like absorption, the quiet taking of a person who stops resisting.

He stood still, letting the quiet press against him.

The day did not pull at him.
And that, he realized, was its own kind of danger.

Kai returned to the house in the early afternoon. The light through the windows rested softly on the floor, unmoving. It made the room feel paused, as if the day were holding still until he decided what to do with it.

He set his keys on the counter.
The sound was quiet.
Almost polite.

Nothing in the house reacted.
Nothing ever did.

He walked into the living room.
A book lay open on the coffee table. He did not remember reading it, but the bookmark sat halfway through as if he had been making steady progress.
He lifted it.

Self-improvement.
Habits.
Structure.

The pages were filled with neat lines he could not recall underlining.
Advice he did not remember accepting.
Rules he had no memory of following.

He set the book down and felt a small tug of confusion, not strong enough to unsettle him, just enough to notice that someone in this life had been trying to become better.

He was not sure it had been him.

On the side table beside the couch sat a small plant in a ceramic pot.
Its leaves were perfectly green.
Perfectly shaped.
Not one brown edge.
Not one torn or wilted piece.

He leaned closer.

There was something strange about it.
It looked exactly as it had that morning.

And the morning before.
And the morning he woke into this life.

Healthy, but unchanged.

A living thing that refused to grow.

He touched one of the leaves lightly.
It did not bend.
It did not resist.
It simply existed, the same shape it had been the
day before, untouched by time or light or care.

A thought brushed through him.
Life can survive without moving forward.
It just cannot become anything new.

He stood and walked to the hallway mirror.
His reflection looked rested, composed, almost
content.
The kind of face people describe as stable.

He studied the eyes.

They were calm, but not with clarity.
Calm in the way a person becomes smooth after
being sanded down for too long.

He touched the frame of the mirror.
The glass felt cool, steady, indifferent.

A strange feeling passed through him, as if the
mirror were showing him not who he was, but who
he agreed to be.

A thought rose inside him with a quiet certainty.
He was not losing himself in this life.
He was fading at the edges.

Not erased.
Not broken.
Just softened into something that required nothing
and expected nothing.

He stepped away and walked to the kitchen.
Opened a cabinet.
Closed it again.

He did not know what he was looking for.
He only knew that he had stopped expecting to find
anything that mattered.

His phone vibrated on the table.

A message from a coworker.
A simple reminder about tomorrow's agenda.

No urgency.
No pressure.
No conversation.

He typed a brief reply.
Thank you.
See you then.

The response felt automatic, the movement of
someone who had learned how to function without
leaving a trace.

He sat down at the table.

The chair did not squeak.
The floor did not shift.
The room did not press or pull.

Everything remained exactly as it had been before
he entered.

He placed his hands flat on the table.
Waited for something to rise inside him.
A thought.
A worry.
A longing.

Nothing came.

He breathed in and realized the air tasted the same
as it had that morning.
Clean.
Even.
Unremarkable.

He felt the thinning again.

A quiet drift inward, like sand slipping through
fingers, like the slow fading of a photograph left too
long in the sun.

He rubbed his thumb against his palm, trying to
ground himself.
The motion felt familiar but not meaningful.

He stood and walked to the window.
Outside, a man trimmed his bushes in slow, deliberate strokes.
Another neighbor stepped out, took in the mail, and returned inside without glancing around.
A child biked past, wheels turning in a perfect rhythm.

Everything matched.
Everything repeated.
Nothing changed.

Kai felt a thought form, soft but sharp enough to hold.

This life did not take anything from him.
It simply gave him nothing to grow against.

He looked back at the plant on the table.

Still perfect.
Still untouched.
Still alive without living.

A quiet reflection of the person he was becoming here.

He placed a hand on the window frame, feeling its smooth surface beneath his palm.

A life without resistance can still erase a person.
Not loudly.
Not violently.
Slowly.

Kindly.
Quietly.

He let his hand fall to his side.

Something inside him wanted to move.
Something inside him wanted to resist the stillness.

But the room stayed steady.
The world stayed steady.
And the version of him living here had already
learned how to stop pushing.

Kai stood in the silence, realizing that this life did
not challenge him, hurt him, or demand anything
from him.

It only asked him to stay the same.

And that, he understood, was the cost.

Kai woke the next morning with no memory of
falling asleep.

No dream.
No thought fading into darkness.
Just a quiet blank where the night should have
been.

He sat up slowly.
Nothing in the room had changed.
The plant on the side table was still perfect.
The horizon print still hung at the exact center of

the wall.
The air still held its measured calm.

He felt something inside him shift.

Not panic.
Not clarity.
A soft confusion, like realizing you forgot a word you once used every day.

He walked into the kitchen.

The apples in the bowl sat exactly as they had the day before.
Three.
Polished.
Arranged with intention.

His coffee machine blinked its steady light.
Waiting.
Predictable.

He pressed the button.
The machine hummed.
The same hum as yesterday.
The same hum as the day before.
The same hum as his first morning in this life.

He lifted the mug to his lips.

The taste was identical.
So identical it felt unnatural.

He lowered the mug and stared at the wall.

For a moment, he could not remember what day it was supposed to be.
Not the number.
Not the date.
The feeling.

Every day carried the same shape.

He walked to the window and opened the curtain.

The man across the street walked his dog again.
The same pace.
The same distance between each step.
The same calm slack in the leash.

Kai watched them pass.

They did not look up.
They did not break rhythm.

His hand tightened around the curtain.

He felt something crack at the edge of his chest.
Not pain.
Not fear.

Recognition.

A life with no friction does not hold a person in place.
It dissolves them.

He closed the curtain, and the room settled back into perfect balance.

Too perfect.

He turned and caught his reflection in the
microwave door.
His face looked steady.
Even rested.

But the eyes were wrong.

They looked like the eyes of someone who had
stopped asking questions.

For a moment, he tried to remember a version of
himself that wanted something, but the memory
slipped through him like water.

He stepped away from the reflection.

He needed to breathe air that felt like something.

He walked outside.

The sky was soft and pale.
Clouds spaced evenly, as if arranged to avoid
drawing attention.
No sharp shadows.
No bright light.

The street was quiet.

Not peaceful quiet.
Not heavy quiet.

Empty quiet.

A bird landed on a branch nearby.
It sat motionless for a long moment, then hopped once and left.
The branch did not sway.

Nothing here moved unless it needed to.

A neighbor waved from a driveway.
The motion was gentle, the expression neutral.

Morning, Kai.

The tone carried no warmth and no distance.
Just recognition.
Recognition without meaning.

Kai raised a hand but did not speak.

He realized something.

Every person he met in this life accepted him.
Welcomed him.
Trusted him.

But no one truly knew him.

Because there was nothing here to reveal him.

No conflict.
No pressure.
No choice.
No chance to become anything.

He walked farther down the sidewalk.

Everything mirrored itself.
Lawns evenly cut.
Mailboxes in perfect alignment.
Cars washed to the same quiet shine.

He felt the air press in around him.

This was a life where a person could live forever without realizing they were gone.

His breath shook, almost imperceptibly.

The shift began.

A soft tilt in the world.
A bending of the light at the edges.
A quiet loosening of reality.

He closed his eyes, bracing himself.

Not out of fear.
Out of the knowledge that if he stayed here any longer, he might never notice the changes inside him again.

The sidewalk felt thinner beneath his feet.
The air warmed in a way that did not match the weather.

He heard a low sound in his chest.

Not a heartbeat.
A realization.

If he stayed here, he would stop wanting.

And once a person stops wanting, they stop becoming.

The shift strengthened.
Reality softened around him.

His last clear thought was a warning to himself, a final trace of the man he had been in other lives.

His last thought before the world let go was simple and quiet.

A life without pain can still destroy a person.
It just takes longer.

Then the world released him, and the life that kept him numb could no longer hold him.

Chapter Eight: The Life That Waited Without Him

Kai woke into quiet.

Not the kind that comforts.
Not the kind that warns.
A neutral quiet.
A quiet that asked nothing of him.

He opened his eyes slowly.

The ceiling above him was smooth and unmarked.
Perfect white.
Perfect stillness.
A surface that had never held a story.

He sat up.

The bed was neatly made except for the space his
body had shaped.
No other warmth.
No other imprint.
Just one life pressing softly into the sheets and
rising again without consequence.

He looked around the room.

Everything was arranged with clean intention.
Muted colors.
Soft lines.
No clutter.

No chaos.
Nothing broken.
Nothing precious.

It was the kind of room someone might choose if
they wanted their life to feel manageable.

A faint calm settled over him.
Not comfort.
Not peace.
Just a soft absence where feelings might have lived.

He stepped into the hallway.

The air moved in a slow, predictable rhythm, as if
the house exhaled on schedule.
The walls were bare except for one framed print.

A horizon line.
Perfectly straight.
Perfectly centered.
So balanced it felt almost unnatural.

Something in him tightened for a moment.
A small flicker.
A brief signal that the room wanted to teach him
something he was not ready to hear.

He walked into the kitchen.

The appliances gleamed.
The counters were spotless.
A fruit bowl held three identical apples, each one

polished as if they had been arranged for display more than for eating.

He picked one up and set it back down.

The bowl did not shift.

Nothing here shifted unless someone intended it to.

He made coffee without thinking.
One scoop.
Water.
Button.

The machine hummed its soft, perfect hum.
A sound without personality.
A sound engineered to never interrupt.

He poured the coffee into a plain white mug.
He lifted it.
He drank.

The taste was fine.
Not good.
Not bad.
Just fine.

He felt the neutrality of it move through him.

For a moment, something inside him pushed against the stillness.
A faint irritation.
A question without words.
A reminder that even numbness has edges.

But the feeling faded quickly, swallowed by the quiet shape of the room.

He walked to the window and pulled back the curtain.

Outside, the neighborhood was washed in soft morning light.
Lawns trimmed.
Cars clean.
No noise.
No rush.
No urgency.

The world sat evenly, like a lake without wind.

A man across the street walked his dog.
The dog trotted at a steady pace.
Never pulling.
Never lagging.
The leash was slack, as if both of them had agreed to remove struggle from their lives.

Kai watched them pass.

They did not look up.
They did not wave.
Not out of rudeness.
Out of rhythm.

Everyone here moved in rhythms that protected them from wanting too much.

He breathed in.
The air felt precise.
Measured.
Like a room that had learned how to regulate itself.

Something shifted inside him.

He realized he could stay here for years and never notice the days passing. That frightened him more than anything he had survived.

He let the curtain fall back into place.

The house waited for him.
Patient.
Unchanging.
Ready to offer him another day that asked nothing and gave nothing.

A day that could repeat forever.

He felt the faintest pull inside his chest.
The smallest reminder of who he had been in other mornings.
It flickered once, then dimmed.

Still, the truth it carried did not vanish.

A life without pain, without chaos, without need, could still take everything from a person.

It could take them slowly.

Quietly.

By giving them nothing to push against.

Kai stood in the center of the room, surrounded by the soft balance of a world designed to keep him steady.

A world that would let him drift until he no longer noticed he was drifting.

He closed his eyes.

The stillness pressed in.

And for the first time in this life, he felt the loneliness inside the calm.

Kai stepped outside, expecting the morning to greet him with some trace of movement.
Instead, the quiet followed him.

The air held no edge.
No shift in temperature.
No hint of change.
It was the sort of morning that could repeat itself without being noticed.

He walked down the path.
The concrete looked clean, almost polished.
The grass on either side was trimmed to an exact height, every blade cut with mechanical precision.

A neighbor across the street watered her plants.
Slowly.

Evenly.
Each pot received the same amount of care, the same rhythm of motion, as if she had practiced it.

She looked up and gave Kai a small nod.

Not warm.
Not cold.
Just enough acknowledgment to maintain the balance of the morning.

He returned the nod.

She went back to watering in the same steady pattern.

He continued walking.

No children rushing to school.
No music leaking from a passing car.
No delivery trucks humming in the distance.

The world here moved at a pace designed to protect itself from disruption.

He reached the corner and paused.

A man on a bicycle approached.
Not fast.
Not slow.
Just steady.

Kai stepped aside, though the man had enough space to pass.

The cyclist nodded without breaking rhythm.

Kai watched him travel down the street, his movements smooth and practiced, almost synchronized with the evenly spaced houses behind him.

For a moment, Kai felt as if he were watching a pattern, not a person.

It struck him that the morning would continue its pattern whether he walked this street or disappeared from it entirely.

He walked on.

A soft breeze brushed his face.
Even the wind here felt measured.
Controlled.
It touched him briefly, then left as if careful not to disturb his thoughts.

He passed a row of homes that looked nearly identical.
Different colors, same shape.
Different plants, same arrangement.

Each yard seemed designed to avoid drawing attention.

He felt the quiet shifting inside him again.

This life was not empty.
It was curated.

It was built to protect someone from longing, from reaching, from wanting more than the world was willing to give.

He stopped at a small park.

A single bench sat beneath a large tree.
The branches above him barely moved, held in the stillness of a morning that refused to change its mind.

He sat.

A moment passed.
Then another.
Each one so soft it barely left a trace.

He looked at his hands.

They rested calmly in his lap.
Steady.
Still.
As if they belonged to someone who had surrendered every sharp desire in exchange for the comfort of predictability.

He exhaled slowly.

The ease of this life was starting to fold around him.

He could feel it.
The gentle pull.
The soft settling.

The quiet suggestion that nothing needed to move if he chose not to.

He realized he could stay here for years and never notice the days passing. That frightened him more than anything he had survived.

A thought rose inside him, quiet but unmistakable.

This was a world that waited for him.
But it did not need him.

He looked around the park again.

Everything was in its place.
Everything was balanced.
Everything was fine.

And fine had a way of erasing a person without ever harming them.

He stood up slowly.

The grass under his shoes held no memory of his steps.

Nothing here held him.
Nothing here released him.

The morning simply accepted him without asking who he was or who he wanted to become.

It felt less like being welcomed and more like being absorbed.

As he walked back toward the house, the quiet trailed behind him, soft as breath.

A life without struggle.
A life without urgency.
A life without friction.

A life that could let him disappear without ever noticing he was gone.

Kai stepped back into the house.

The door closed behind him with a soft click.
Not loud.
Not sharp.
Just enough sound to remind him he had crossed from one stillness into another.

The air inside felt warmer than the morning outside.
Not comforting.
Not heavy.
Simply warm in a way that suggested the room cared more about temperature than about him.

He walked through the living room.

Nothing had changed.
Nothing ever changed here.
The furniture sat exactly where it always sat.
Not a pillow out of place.
Not a book left open.

Not a single sign that anyone lived in the room long enough to disturb it.

He touched the back of the couch.

The fabric felt smooth.
Too smooth.
As if it had never absorbed the shape of a tired body at the end of a long day.

He moved into the kitchen.

His mug from earlier still sat on the counter.
Centered.
Balanced.
Unbothered by time.

He lifted it.

The coffee inside had cooled, but it looked untouched, as if the room did not allow its warmth to change without permission.

He set it down again.

The house felt like it was holding a breath it never intended to release.

He could not shake the sense that it had been holding that breath long before he ever woke up in it.

Kai walked to the window above the sink.
The street outside was quiet.
The same quiet.

The kind that wrapped itself around a person until they forgot how silence was supposed to feel.

He watched a car roll by at a perfect speed.
Not rushed.
Not slow.
Perfect.

The world here seemed designed to prevent urgency.

He turned away from the window.

A small stack of mail sat on the counter.
Every envelope aligned.
No bends.
No tears.
It looked arranged, not delivered.

He picked one up.

His name printed neatly.
Centered.
Even the font felt calm.

He placed it back in the stack.

The stillness in the room pressed a little closer.

He walked down the hallway.
The air cooled slightly.
Not enough to provoke discomfort.
Just enough to keep him awake.

He reached the bedroom and paused in the doorway.

The bed he had left earlier was made again.
Perfect corners.
Smooth blanket.
No sign that a body had ever rested there.

He had no memory of making it.

He stepped inside.

The faint scent of fresh linen clung to the air, clean and neutral.
A scent chosen by someone who wanted a space to feel simple, not intimate.

He sat on the edge of the bed.

The mattress did not dip the way a used bed should.
It held him lightly, as if waiting to decide whether he belonged there.

For a moment, he felt a question rise inside him.

A quiet one.
The kind that arrives only when a room is too calm to hide it.

Was this comfort or absence?

He did not know.

He only knew the room felt like it would remain exactly itself if he vanished.

He realized the house was not keeping him safe. It was keeping him small.

But he knew the room would not answer.

He leaned forward, elbows on his knees, hands clasped loosely.

The silence pressed in.
Not aggressively.
Not painfully.
Just persistently.
Like a thought that kept repeating itself because no other thoughts were loud enough to interrupt.

He stared at the floor.

The wood shone softly.
No scratches.
No dents.
No history.

He felt something shift inside him.
A small, steady awareness.

This was a life without friction.
A life that removed every sharp corner.
A life that offered nothing to push against.

And without something to push against, a person could forget they existed.

He stood slowly.

The quiet followed him.

It always did.

He walked to the mirror on the wall.

His reflection stared back.
Unchanged.
Untouched.

But the eyes were different.

Softer.
Dimmer.
Like a flame kept low for too long.

The face looking back did not seem missing from this life. It seemed optional.

He reached out and touched the glass.

His fingers left no print.

The room erased even that.

He stepped back.

The house waited.

Still.
Balanced.
Perfect.

And for the first time, the perfection felt like a warning.

Chapter Nine: The Life He Was Meant to Live

Kai woke into warmth.

Not comfort.
Not ease.
A grounded warmth.
The kind that felt earned instead of arranged.

Light moved across the room in slow, natural strokes.
Nothing in it was staged.
Nothing was curated.
It felt lived in, gently, honestly.

He sat up.

The sheets carried the faint scent of someone who slept beside him often enough to leave a softness in the air. Not perfume. Not artificial. Something human. Something real.

Why did this place feel like something he lost instead of something he found?

He looked around the bedroom.

It was not perfect.
It was not polished.
It was not designed to keep him steady.

It was a room that held a life, not an image.

A sweater draped over a chair.
A half-read book on the nightstand.
A window cracked just enough to let the morning in.

Nothing forced.
Nothing balanced to hide a truth.

He felt something shift inside him.
Not confusion.
Not fear.

Recognition.

The quiet kind that does not ask questions because it already knows the answers.

He felt the first real sense of belonging he had experienced in any version of himself.

He stood and moved through the hallway.
There were photos on the walls—no gloss, no staging, no symmetry.
Moments caught because someone cared enough to hold them.

A hand on his shoulder in one picture.
A laugh he could almost hear in another.
A sunset behind two silhouettes whose closeness was unmistakable.

He touched one frame lightly.

The version of him in the photo looked... present.
Not drained.
Not numb.
Not holding a world together.
Not disappearing into ease.

Present.

Something in the morning felt borrowed, as if he had stepped into a life that expected him to remember it.

He stepped into the kitchen.

A mug sat by the sink, a small chipped line near the rim.
A pan on the stove, still cooling.
A plant by the window that looked like it had been rescued from dying more than once.

The room held a rhythm he recognized inside his chest even if he could not name the memories.

This was not the life he escaped into.
This was not the life that trapped him.
This was not the life that praised him.
This was not the life that drained him.

This was the life he *showed up for*.

He felt it immediately.

Not perfect.
Not dramatic.
Not demanding.

Aligned.

The kind of alignment that does not announce itself.
It simply fits.

A quiet thought rose inside him, sharp and soft at
the same time:

This life had not abandoned him.
He had abandoned it.

Another thought followed, heavier:

And he remembered why.

Not fully.
Not clearly.

But the ache arrived before the memory did.

He leaned against the counter and let the truth
settle.

The room did not hold him together.
The room did not hold him captive.
The room simply reflected a version of him he barely
recognized anymore.

A version he had once worked toward.

A version he had once trusted.

A version he had once believed he could become.

And for a brief moment, the weight of that recognition pressed into him with a quiet devastation.

This was the life he was meant to live.

Not because it was easy.
Not because it was beautiful.

But because it told the truth about who he really was.

And who he had stopped being.

Kai stepped outside into a morning that did not try to impress him.

The air was cool, real, carrying the faint smell of rain that had not fallen yet.
The sky was open in a way he had not felt in any other life.
Not curated.
Not controlled.
Not edited into calm.

He walked down the steps slowly.

The wood creaked beneath his weight, a small sound that felt more alive than the silence he had lived in before. A leaf blew across the yard, scraping lightly along the concrete. The world here moved in imperfect rhythms.

A car drove by with a soft rattle in the engine.
A dog barked down the street.
A child's laughter cut through the morning, sudden and bright.

Nothing about it was balanced.
Nothing about it was arranged.
And the lack of perfection made something inside him unclench.

A neighbor waved from across the street.

Her wave was warm but distracted, the way people wave when they are busy living.
He raised a hand in return.

She smiled and shouted, "Tell her I left the dish on the porch!"
Then she disappeared back into her house before he could ask who "her" was.

The world here assumed he belonged.
It assumed he knew the stories, the routines, the spaces that held his life.

He walked toward the sidewalk.

The pavement was cracked in one corner, weeds pushing through in stubborn lines.
He stopped for a moment, looking at the uneven ground.

A life with cracks.
A life that kept growing anyway.

Further down the street, he saw an older man adjusting a crooked mailbox. The man looked up when Kai approached.

"Morning," the man said, wiping sweat from his forehead.
"You fixing that again?" Kai heard himself ask.

The familiarity in his own voice startled him.

"Storm knocked it loose last week," the man replied. "You told me you would help me reinforce it once things settled at home."

Kai nodded slowly.
The words settled in his chest.

Once things settled at home.

He did not know what storm had hit his life here.
He did not know what had come undone.
He only knew that this version of him had been trying to hold something together long before he arrived.

He helped the man lift the post, holding it steady as the man tightened the bolts. When they finished, the man smiled.

"See," he said. "Still standing."

"Most things do," Kai answered quietly.

"Not on their own," the man corrected.

The words stayed with him long after Kai walked away.

He turned the corner toward the small park. The grass was uneven, dotted with patches that needed tending. A couple sat on a bench, talking in low tones. A teenager practiced free throws at the far end of the court, missing more than he made. A jogger ran by with uneven breaths, slowing, then speeding up again.

Nothing was smooth here.

Nothing was perfected.

Nothing hid its effort.

And something about that truthfulness made his chest tighten.

He sat on an empty bench.

For a moment, he let the morning settle around him.

This was a life shaped by attempts.

By repairs.

By growth that had not yet found its final form.

He felt the ache rise again, sharper this time.

This life was not asking him to escape it.

It was asking him to face it.

And facing it meant remembering why he had left.

He closed his eyes.
The warmth of the morning touched his skin gently,
as if the world was still willing to welcome him back.

He realized this life had been waiting for him to
return, and the fear in his chest came from knowing
he was the one who walked away.

But even in that warmth, he felt the shadow of
something else.
A truth waiting.
A memory approaching.
A reason he had not yet seen.

The life he was meant to live was calling him home.

But the cost of coming back had not revealed itself
yet.

Kai reached the end of the street and stopped.

A small workshop stood at the corner, its door
cracked open just enough to let the morning spill
across the floor. Wooden shelves lined the walls.
Tools hung with no sense of display or perfection.
Everything here looked used, repaired, repurposed.
Nothing staged. Nothing wasted.

He stepped inside.

The air smelled of cedar and something warm, like a life shaped with hands instead of habits.

On the workbench sat a half-finished project. A frame of some kind. Smooth corners. Sanded edges. A form that was becoming something but had not yet decided what.

He touched it lightly.

For a moment he felt something unusual. Not a memory. Something deeper. A muscle memory of intention. As if he had built this piece a thousand times in another version of himself.

A man stepped out from the back room.

Older. Strong hands. A quiet face. Not surprised to see him.

"There you are," he said. "I wondered if you would come in this morning."

Kai froze slightly.

You know me?

The man nodded in a slow, steady way.

"Better than you think."

Kai looked at the unfinished frame again.

What is this.

The man wiped his hands on a cloth.

Something you started. Something you did not finish yet. You said you would know when it was time to come back to it.

Kai felt the truth press softly against him. He did not know the project. But it knew him.

The man studied him with a patience that carried years inside it.

"You left for a while, he said. That happens. People forget where they belong. They forget what they were building.

Kai swallowed. His voice felt thin in his throat.

"Why did I leave?"

The man did not answer right away. He walked to the bench, tightened a clamp on the wooden frame, and spoke quietly.

Leaving is not the question. Anyone can leave. What matters is why you stayed gone.

The words landed like something Kai had been circling without seeing.

He stepped closer.

Do you know me in this life?

The man met his eyes.

I know the version of you who stopped running from himself.

And it scared Kai how much he wanted to meet that man again.

He felt a sting of fear, sharp and honest, that the man remembered a version of him he was no longer sure he could return to.

The one who built instead of escaped. The one who did not hide behind busyness or belonging or control.

Kai felt something shift inside him. A truth rising that he was not ready to hold.

The man continued.

"You were becoming someone here. Someone honest. Someone aligned. Someone willing to do the work that hurts before it heals."

Kai looked down at the unfinished frame again.

"What work?"

The man smiled gently, not as a teacher, but as someone who had seen this moment before.

"Your own."

He placed a hand on the frame.

"You said once that purpose is not found. It is built. Piece by piece. Day by day. Choice by choice. You knew that here."

Kai felt the ache return. Soft. Deep.

If this was the life he was meant to live, then somewhere inside him was the reason he left.

The man stepped aside.

"Finish it when you are ready. I will be here."

Kai ran his fingers along the wood one more time.

It felt right in his hands.

It felt like something he had lost.

It felt like something that had been waiting for him.

And for the first time, he understood the truth he had been circling since morning.

Purpose was not a destination.

It was who you chose to become when no one was watching.

He stepped back toward the door.

The workshop did not pull him forward or push him away. It simply waited, the same way this life had been waiting for him.

He lingered for a moment.

Then he stepped outside, carrying the quiet weight of a life he had once chosen and somehow walked away from.

And he knew now that this life was not asking him to return; it was preparing him for what he still had to face.

Chapter Ten: The Confrontation With the Self

Kai woke into the same warmth he felt before.
The same room.
The same soft light moving across the walls.
Nothing had shifted around him, yet everything felt different.

It wasn't the same life returning, just the same room, borrowed one final time to show him what he still refused to face.

He sat up slowly.
The sheets held the same faint scent, human and familiar, but it no longer felt like a life he was returning to.
It felt like a life he was passing through.

He looked around the room.
The sweater on the chair.
The half-read book.
The window cracked open to the morning air.
All of it belonged to a version of him who once knew how to stay.

He realized he had not come back to live in this life.
He had come back to face something it could no longer hide from him.

Recognition rose in him again, but this time it carried consequence.
Not comfort.
Not belonging.
A summons.

The quiet kind that does not ask questions because it already knows the answers.

He stood and moved through the hallway.
There were photos on the walls, no gloss, no staging, no symmetry.
Moments caught because someone cared enough to hold them.

A hand on his shoulder in one picture.
A laugh he could almost hear in another.
A sunset behind two silhouettes whose closeness was unmistakable.

He touched one frame lightly.
The version of him in the photo looked present.
Not drained.
Not numb.
Not holding a world together.
Not disappearing into ease.
Present.

He stepped into the kitchen.

A mug sat by the sink, a small chipped line near the rim.
A pan on the stove, still cooling.

A plant by the window that looked like it had been rescued from dying more than once.

The room held a rhythm he recognized inside his chest, even if he could not name the memories.

This was not the life he escaped into.
This was not the life that trapped him.
This was not the life that praised him.
This was not the life that drained him.

This was the life he showed up for.

He felt it immediately.
Not perfect.
Not dramatic.
Not demanding.
Aligned.

The kind of alignment that does not announce itself.
It simply fits.

A quiet thought rose inside him, sharp and soft at the same time:
He had not been taken from this life.
He had walked away from it.

Another thought followed, heavier:
And he remembered why.
Not fully.
Not clearly.
But the ache arrived before the memory did.

He leaned against the counter and let the truth settle.

The room did not hold him together.
The room did not hold him captive.
The room reflected a man he barely recognized anymore.

A version he had once worked toward.
A version he had once trusted.
A version he had once believed he could become.

And for a brief moment, the weight of that recognition pressed into him with a quiet devastation.

This was the life he was meant to live.
Not because it was easy.
Not because it was beautiful.
But because it told the truth about who he really was.
And who he had stopped being.

He stepped forward.

The air thickened, then thinned, as if preparing to reveal something he had avoided across every life he slipped through.

The world around him softened.
Edges blurred.
Light dimmed, then brightened again.

When the fog cleared, he was standing on smooth stone.
Bare feet.
Cool surface.
A path stretching into the kind of emptiness that demands an answer.

This was no life.
No world.
No version.

This was the place between them.

It felt like standing inside the pause between two heartbeats.

He walked forward.

The fog shifted, clearing just enough to show a bench made from the same stone as the ground.

A man sat on it.

Kai stopped breathing for a moment.

He knew the shape of those shoulders.
He knew the quiet way those hands folded.
He knew the stillness of that posture.

It was him.

Not older.
Not younger.
Not different.
Him.

Kai felt a quiet panic rising, not from the world he had entered, but from the truth he knew he could no longer outrun.

The version without a life attached.
The version without a world wrapped around him.
The version without distraction.

His own eyes lifted to meet his.

Calm.
Steady.
Unimpressed by every life he had run to.

The other Kai spoke first.

"You finally made it."

The voice did not echo.
The world absorbed it, as if it belonged here.

Kai stepped forward, though every part of him resisted.

"What is this?"

The other self gestured to the emptiness around them.

"The place where you cannot run."

The fog curled at their feet, patient, waiting.

"You think the worlds are changing," the other said quietly.
"They are not."

Kai swallowed.

"You are the one shifting. The lives just reveal where you break."

The words sank into him with slow certainty.

This was not a life he could escape.
This was not a version he could drift through.
This was the truth he had outrun in every life he touched.

He lowered himself onto the stone bench beside his other self.

For the first time since the first life slipped, there was nowhere to go.

There was only him.

And the truth he had avoided long enough.

The confrontation had begun.

They sat in silence.

Not the comfortable kind.
Not the strained kind.
A silence shaped for truth.

Kai kept his hands still on his knees.
His other self watched him with the patience of someone who had already lived the moment many times.

Finally, the other Kai spoke.

"You think you are lost because the worlds keep shifting."
A pause.
"You are lost because you keep shifting."

Kai looked down at the ground.
The stone felt solid, but his own presence felt unsteady.
He breathed slowly, trying to steady a tremor he could not name.

"You left every life because it did not feel like you," the other continued.
"Did it ever occur to you that the lives were never the problem?"

Silence again.
Heavy.
Precise.

Kai swallowed hard.

"Then what is the problem?"

His other self leaned back slightly, as if giving the truth room to move.

"You have never learned how to stay."

The sentence landed heavier than any world he had left behind.

The words hit him with a quiet force.
Not loud.
Not dramatic.
Just true.

"You stay until it gets heavy.
You stay until it gets honest.
You stay until you recognize yourself.
Then you run."

Kai felt the sting of that.
Not betrayal.
Recognition.

"I did not run," he said softly.

The other self studied him, unimpressed.

"You ran from Mira.
You ran from discipline.
You ran from duty.
You ran from belonging.
You ran from the life you were meant to live."

The memory of that life flickered at the edge of his mind, distant, unfinished, still carrying a weight he had never resolved.

Kai clenched his jaw.

"I did what I had to do."

The fog shifted at the edges of the path, swirling slowly, as if the world were agreeing with him.

"You did what felt familiar," his other self answered. "You abandoned yourself the moment you felt seen."

Kai looked away.

Every life he had slipped through rose in his mind.
The woman who loved him.
The life that praised him.
The life that drained him.
The life that numbed him.
The life that depended on him.
The life that needed his discipline.
The life that reflected his deepest fear.
The life that reflected his deepest potential.

Every single one revealed something.
Every single one exposed something.

His other self continued.

"You did not lose those lives.
You walked away from them because they showed you who you were becoming."

Kai felt something unravel in his chest.

"Then what am I becoming?"

His other self did not soften.

"Someone who knows how to move.
Someone who knows how to shift.
But not someone who knows how to choose."

That cut deeper than anything else.

"You keep thinking your purpose is waiting in one of the worlds you entered," the other said.
"It is not."

Kai looked up slowly.

"Then where is it?"

His other self pointed to him.
Not dramatically.
Not symbolically.
Simply and plainly.

"In the version of you that stops running."

The fog thinned for a moment, revealing glimpses of every life he had passed through.
Places he had slept.
Faces he had touched.
Mornings, he had escaped.

Then the fog closed again.

Kai felt the weight of it settling into him.

"Why show me all these lives?" he whispered.

His other self looked at him with steady calm.

"Because you needed to see every version of yourself.
The ambitious one.
The numb one.
The loved one.
The drained one.
The disciplined one.
The useful one.
The one who broke.
The one who healed.
The one who disappeared.
The one who belonged."

Kai felt tears rise, not from sadness, but from the overwhelming truth of it.

"You needed to meet every version," the other said, "so you could decide which one you will stop abandoning."

In that moment, he understood that he had never been searching for the right life. He had been searching for a version of himself he would not abandon.

Every world had been a mirror. He had been the one looking away.

The world went silent again.

Kai sat with that.

He had spent so long searching for the life that fit.

He had never asked if he fit inside himself.

The other Kai leaned forward slightly.

"This next moment will not be about the worlds.
It will be about you."

Kai breathed in slowly.

He understood what came next.
He understood what he could no longer avoid.
He understood why every life slipped just when he
wanted to stay.

The world waited.

The truth waited.

The choice waited.

The confrontation was not finished.

It was about to deepen.

The world around them shifted.

Not violently.
Not suddenly.
With the slow inevitability of a truth that had waited
long enough.

The fog began to thin, revealing fragments of the
lives Kai had slipped through.

A doorway here.
A kitchen there.
A woman at a table.
A life held together by effort.
A life held together by discipline.
A life held together by love.
A life held together by nothing at all.

Each fragment hovered at the edge of sight, never fully forming, never fully fading.

Kai watched them circle him like quiet satellites.

His other self stood now.

"You wanted the worlds to choose you," he said. "They never could. They only showed you who you were in each one."

Kai felt something inside him bracing for impact.

His other self stepped closer.

"In Mira's life, you learned what honesty costs.
In the disciplined life, you learned what control costs.
In the life of repair, you learned what being needed costs.
In the life where you belonged, you learned what love costs.
In the quiet life, you learned what comfort costs."

The fragments around them brightened one by one.

"You saw every way a life can shape you.
What you never asked was how you shape the life."

Kai swallowed, the weight of that truth settling into his chest.

His other self looked directly into his eyes.

"You keep leaving because you think each life is missing something.
The truth is simpler.
You were missing something."

Kai felt the sting of that land deeper than any accusation.

He spoke quietly.

"What was I missing?"

His other self did not hesitate.

"Choice."

The world fell still.

"You moved through lives without choosing who you were in them.
You drifted.
You adjusted.
You reacted.
You escaped.
You survived.
But you did not choose."

Kai felt something tightening behind his ribs.
A pressure that had been growing since the first shift.

His other self continued.

"You are here because the world cannot give you your purpose.
You are here because you must give your purpose to the world."

The fog drew back further, revealing a blank horizon.

Empty.
Ready.
Waiting.

Every life had shown him the same pattern, movement without choice.

"This is the life between lives," the other said.

There were no props here. No roles. Only the weight of who he had been and who he could still become.

"The place where you decide what kind of man will walk forward.
Not what world you want.
What version of yourself you will carry?"

Kai felt his breath catch.

"So I must choose who I am?"

His other self nodded slowly.

"And once you choose, the next life will not slip.
You will not run.
You will not fracture.
You will not search for yourself across different versions."

A long silence stretched between them.

Then his other self spoke with a softness that surprised him.

"I am not here to tell you which version to become.
I am here because you must face the one thing you avoided in every life."

Kai's voice was barely a whisper.

"What is that?"

His other self stepped closer until they were inches apart.

"Your responsibility to yourself."

The world around them brightened, the fog pulling upward like a curtain being lifted.

Kai felt the shift coming.

Not the involuntary pull of the past nine lives.
A different pull.
A pull that waited for his permission.

He looked at his other self.

"What happens if I choose wrong?"

The other Kai smiled, not with confidence, but with gentleness.

"There is no wrong choice.
There is only the choice you refuse to make."

Kai closed his eyes.

The lives flickered around him.
Mira's steady voice.
The disciplined life's order.
The repair life's weight.
The warmth of someone who once chose him.
The quiet life's stillness.
The aligned life's truth.

One question rose above all others.

Who am I willing to carry forward?

The ground warmed beneath his feet.

The shift gathered its strength.

Kai opened his eyes.

For a moment, he felt the instinct to run flicker inside him, the last ghost of the man he used to be.

"I am ready."

His other self stepped back.

"Then choose."

The world paused.

Every version of Kai waited for the decision of the man standing in the center of all of them.

He took a breath.

He chose.

The world dissolved in silence.

And Kai fell into the life that would no longer let him run.

For the first time, he did not fear where he was going, only who he was finally becoming.

Chapter Eleven: The Return to the Chosen Life

Kai landed on his feet.

Not harshly.
Not softly.
As if the world had placed him down with intention.

Grass brushed against his shoes.
A breeze moved across his face with a warmth that
felt familiar but not entirely claimed.
Light filtered through leaves above him, shifting in
slow patterns across the ground.

He stood still and let the world settle around him.

No fog.
No fractured memories.
No lives pulling at him from the edges of sight.

Just a morning.

A real one.

He looked down.
His hands were steady.
His breathing was calm.
There was no echo of another version inside his
chest.

This life was not chosen for him.
This life was not handed to him.
This life was not an escape or a distraction.

This was the life shaped by his choice.

The steadiness in his body felt unfamiliar, like
wearing a truth he had avoided long enough.

He took a small step forward.

Nothing slipped.
Nothing bent.
Nothing blurred.

For the first time since the first shift, the ground
beneath him stayed still.

A sound rose in the distance.
Laughter.
Not loud.
Not forced.
A simple morning sound that belonged to people
already awake and living.

He followed the path through the trees.

The air carried a sense he had not felt in any other
life.
Not numbness.
Not pressure.
Not yearning.
Not fragmentation.

Presence.

Each step felt like a quiet agreement between him and the world.

As he reached the end of the path, the trees opened into a small open field.
A street sat beyond it, lined with familiar houses.
Not perfect.
Not polished.
Not curated.

Lived in.

And something inside him recognized the rhythm before he recognized the scenery.

He had been here before.

Not in another version.
Not in another life.
In memory.

He felt a quiet fear move through him, the fear that this might be the life he wanted and the one he no longer deserved.

This was the place he had walked away from.
The life he once lived without understanding its value.

A figure stood by the gate of a nearby house.

Back turned.
Posture familiar in a way that tightened something inside his chest.

The figure turned.

Her.

The woman from the aligned life.
The life he was meant to live.

Her eyes widened in a quiet, stunned recognition.

"Kai."

The word left her lips with softness and certainty, as if she had spoken it a thousand times and was still learning how much it meant.

He felt the morning steady around him.

This was not belonging as a distraction.
This was not love as escape.
This was not comfort as numbing.
This was not effort as survival.

This was the life where he had once been present.
The life he had walked away from.
The life waiting to see who he had become.

He stepped closer.

She did not move away.
She did not rush toward him.

She simply stood still, letting the truth shape the space between them.

"You came back," she said softly.

Kai nodded.

"I chose to."

Saying it out loud made the choice feel heavier, as if the world had just heard a promise it intended to hold him to.

Her expression changed.
Not relief.
Not fear.
A quiet understanding.

She walked toward him slowly, stopping an arm's length away.

"Then this time," she said, "show me the version of you who stays."

The morning held its breath.

And Kai realized this was not the reunion.

This was the beginning.

Kai stepped into the living room slowly as if the air itself held pieces of a truth he had forgotten.
Nothing here felt staged.

Nothing felt borrowed.
Everything carried the quiet weight of a life lived
with intention.

A blanket rested on the arm of the couch, folded
but not perfect.
A pair of slippers sat near the fireplace, one slightly
turned as if someone had slipped out of them in a
moment of distraction.
A stack of letters sat on a small wooden table,
opened and placed in a way that suggested honest
routines rather than curated order.

He moved toward the shelf near the window.
Photographs lined the wood.
Not arranged for presentation.
Arranged for remembering.

He picked one up.

It showed him and the woman from the kitchen.
Their hands intertwined.
Not posed.
Not forced.
A natural closeness, easy and unguarded.

He studied the picture.

The man he used to be stood in front of him.
Not the version that drifted.
Not the version that chased.
Not the version that hid inside achievement or
comfort.
A man who tried.

Even when he was tired.
Even when he doubted himself.

A small ache pressed into his chest.

He put the photo down gently.

Another frame caught his attention.
A candid moment.
Him laughing.
Her looking at him with a softness shaped by trust and time.

He felt it instantly.

Recognition without clarity.
Memory without sequence.
Meaning without shape.

He touched the edge of the frame with his thumb.

He could feel the echo of the man he had been, and the distance between them hurt more than he expected.

The gap between who he was and who he remembered being felt like its own kind of grief.

This was not the life that happened to him.
This was the life he had built.
And broken.
And walked away from before he understood what he was losing.

He stepped back and let his eyes move across the room.

The imperfections.
The warmth.
The lived-in truth of it.

It felt like standing inside a promise he had once believed he could keep.

A quiet breath left him.

He whispered into the stillness, not expecting an answer.

"I knew this place. I just forgot how to stay."

Kai stepped outside, letting the door close softly behind him.
The air carried a sharpness the house did not.
Not cold.
Not punishing.
Just honest.

He stood on the small porch and looked out at the street.
Nothing extraordinary waited for him.
No sign.
No shift in the world bending toward revelation.
Just a morning that belonged to the life he had abandoned.

He walked down the steps slowly.

The path beneath him was uneven.
A crack ran through the middle, filled with dirt and stubborn weeds.
He felt a strange gratitude for it.
It was the first imperfection he had seen in any life that felt real.

A neighbor across the street raised a hand.
The gesture was small and familiar.
Not polite.
Not distant.
Recognizing.

Kai returned it before he realized he had done so.

As he walked farther, his breath settled into a steadier rhythm.
Nothing here was curated to keep him calm.
Nothing here was designed to protect him from himself.
The world simply met him as it was.

He passed a yard where a bike lay on its side.
Someone had left it there the night before without care for symmetry or order.
A dog barked inside a nearby house.
A mailbox leaned slightly from years of being opened with force.
Life here carried friction.

He felt the tension in his shoulders ease.

As he reached the end of the block, a thought rose quietly inside him.
Not a revelation.
Not a memory.
A truth.

He had been capable of building something real before he ever began drifting between lives.
He had been someone worth coming back to.

He stopped on the sidewalk and looked up at the sky.
Clouds moved slowly overhead.
Not perfect shapes.
Not arranged.
Just clouds doing what clouds do.

The simplicity grounded him.

He breathed in and felt it land.

He had not returned to this life to correct a mistake. He had returned because something in him still believed he could become the man this life expected him to be.

For the first time, expectation did not feel like a weight. It felt like an invitation.

He realized he was not stepping back into a life. He was stepping back into himself.

He let the quiet settle around him.
Not the quiet that numbs or erases.
A quiet that clears space.

He turned back toward the house.
Its imperfections did not diminish when he looked
at them again.
If anything, they felt more honest.

He stepped toward the front door with a slow,
steady certainty.
Not because he understood everything.
Not because he remembered everything.
But because this was the first life that felt like a
choice he could make without losing himself.

He reached for the handle.
His hand trembled slightly.
Not from fear.
From recognition.

He opened the door and stepped inside.
The air greeted him with warmth that did not
demand anything from him.

For the first time, he did not feel like a visitor in his
own life.

He felt like someone finally coming home.

This time, home was not the place. It was the
version of himself he refused to leave behind.

Chapter Twelve: The Life He Chose to See

Kai woke into quiet that felt different from any quiet he had met before.
Not curated.
Not controlled.
Not softened for his comfort.

A real quiet.

The kind that comes from a world that is still moving even when you are not.

Light pressed gently against the edges of the room.
Not dramatic.
Not symbolic.
Just morning doing what morning does.

He sat up slowly.

The sheets beneath him were plain.
The pillow carried no unfamiliar imprint.
The air held no hint of another life asking him to belong.

He was back.

Not drifting.
Not suspended between versions of himself.
Not caught in a world that wanted to keep him still.

Back in the life he had left without realizing it.

The world had not reset for him while he was gone;
it had simply continued without his permission.

He looked around the room.

It was imperfect.
A stack of papers leaning near the desk.
A shirt hanging over the back of a chair.
A faint ring on the nightstand where a cup had
been set down too quickly.

Nothing here was arranged to soothe him.
Nothing here tried to protect him.
Nothing here tried to define him.

The room simply waited for him to exist inside it.

He stood.

His legs felt unsteady, as if they remembered all the
places he had walked but had forgotten which one
belonged to him.

He stepped into the hallway.

The light was uneven.
One bulb flickered at the end.
The carpet held a small stain he vaguely
remembered promising himself he would clean.

The world he had returned to carried no illusion.

No perfection.
No applause.
No curated ease.

Only truth.

He reached the living room.

A single plant by the window leaned slightly to one side.
It was not dying, but it was not thriving either.
It looked like something that needed attention from someone who cared enough to give it.

Kai stood in front of it and let the moment settle.

This room did not offer escape.
It did not offer clarity.
It did not offer belonging.

It offered something harder.

A chance.

The chance to face what he had been running from.
The chance to rebuild what had slipped out of alignment.
The chance to become the person all those other lives had tried to imitate.

He felt a shift inside him.
Not the drifting kind.
Not the kind that pulled him away.
The kind that brought him back into himself.

For the first time since the world began to move beneath him, he understood something simple.

He had not been searching for the right life.
He had been searching for the right version of himself to live it.

And now the world, imperfect and unbalanced and unfinished, waited for him to decide who that was going to be.

He exhaled slowly.

He felt the quiet differently now. It no longer frightened him. It waited for him to become someone he could stay with.

The quiet held steady.

This time, it did not swallow him.

It steadied him.

He understood the quiet was not his enemy; it was the mirror he had spent years refusing to look into.

Kai stepped outside.
The air met him with a softness he had not felt in any of the other lives.

Not silence.
Not calm.
Something closer to honesty.

The sky held a muted blue, thin clouds drifting in slow shapes.
Nothing dramatic.
Nothing meant to teach him anything.
Just a morning that existed because mornings always had.

He walked down the steps and felt the weight of his body settle in a way that surprised him.
Grounded.
Present.
Unhidden.

The street was familiar.
Not perfect.
Not curated.
A cracked sidewalk.
A mailbox leaning slightly.
A car with dust along the bumper.

It was a world that had not shaped itself for him.
It simply waited for him to show up.

Participation, he realized, was not about controlling the world but about allowing himself to be fully visible inside it.

A neighbor across the street lifted a hand.
Not a wave of expectation.
Not a greeting of routine.
Something smaller.
A simple acknowledgment of another person being alive at the same time.

Kai nodded back.

He continued down the block.
The houses stood close, not identical, not balanced,
each one shaped by the lives inside them.
Gardens half-tended.
Curtains slightly uneven.
A bicycle left on a lawn by someone who probably
meant to put it away last night.

He felt no resistance here.
No demand.
No disguised hunger pulling at him.

He reached the corner and stopped.

Cars passed.
People walked dogs.
Someone jogged by with a pace that belonged to
their own rhythm, not to a world designed to hold
still.

For the first time in a long time, he felt the world
move without leaving him behind.

He closed his eyes for a moment.

A thought rose with quiet certainty.

He had seen lives that wanted to protect him.
He had seen lives that wanted to use him.
He had seen lives that wanted to love him.
He had seen lives that wanted to hold him in place.

But this life, imperfect and unpolished, asked him for something different.

It asked him to participate.
To choose.
To become.

He opened his eyes.

The street had not changed.
The morning had not shifted.

But he knew he had. He could never return to the version of himself who thought life happened to him instead of through him.

But he felt a steadiness in himself that had been missing in every other version of his life.

Not confidence.
Not certainty.
Presence.

He took another step forward.
Then another.
The ground felt real beneath his shoes.

No illusion.
No escape.
No disguise.

A life he could live in was not waiting for him.

It was waiting for him to begin.

Kai walked until the world quieted again.

Not the quiet of numbness.
Not the quiet of avoidance.
A quieter quiet.
One that waited for him rather than pulled him.

He reached a small hill overlooking the town.
The sky stretched wide above him, open and
indifferent.
The kind of sky that did not promise meaning.
The kind that allowed meaning to arrive on its own.

He sat in the grass.

The blades bent softly under his weight, not
resisting, not welcoming.
Just adjusting.
The way the world adjusts when a person finally
stops running.

A breeze moved through the field.

Not gentle.
Not harsh.
Honest.

He watched the town below him.
The roofs.
The roads.
The shifting lines of people moving through their
morning.

Nothing extraordinary.
Nothing symbolic.
Just life continuing in its steady rhythm.

For a moment, he felt the instinct to leave rise in him.
Then he felt it fade, slow and certain, the way an old fear fades when it realizes it no longer has a home.

He exhaled.

The breath felt different.
Not lighter.
Not heavier.
More his.

A single truth arrived with a clarity he did not resist.

He was not choosing between lives.
He was choosing himself.

Not the version he had performed.
Not the version others needed.
Not the version each world tried to shape.

The one that had been quiet inside him the entire time.

And choosing himself meant accepting that no life would spare him from the work of staying.

He leaned back on his hands and let the sky fill his view.
The light shifted slightly across the clouds.

Not a sign.
Not a message.
Just movement.

Real movement.

Something inside him matched that motion.
Something that had been still for too long.

He closed his eyes and felt a calm settle in his chest.
Not the calm of perfection or balance or safety.
A calm shaped by acceptance.

The world did not bend.
The air did not pull.
The ground did not shift.

Nothing changed around him.

But something in him had stopped breaking.

He opened his eyes.

A new stillness lived there.
Not the stillness of surrender.
The stillness of someone who finally knows which
direction to take.

The morning waited.
Not for his answer.
For his next step.

And he knew he was ready to move.

The only life that mattered now was the one he was willing to walk all the way through.

He realized the lesson was never about the worlds he entered. It was about the man he kept abandoning.

Kai took a step forward, not into a world that promised clarity or certainty, but into one that finally asked him to stay long enough to become who he was meant to be. The morning opened around him, unpolished and unashamed, and he walked into it with a steadiness he had never carried before. The world did not shift this time. He did.

Epilogue: The Life He Finally Met

Kai stood in the doorway of the workshop.

Morning light reached across the room in long, familiar strokes, warming the unfinished frame he had once abandoned. The scent of cedar lingered in the air, steady and honest, the kind of smell that stays long after the hands that shaped it are gone.

He stepped inside.

No shift followed him.
No world bent.
Nothing waited to pull him away.

He picked up the frame.

It felt right in his hands, not because he remembered building it, but because he finally recognized the man who had started it. He guided the plane across the wood. A thin curl fell to the floor.

Simple.
Steady.
His.

Outside, the morning moved without urgency.
Inside, he kept shaping the frame, piece by piece, choosing himself with every pass of the blade.

When he finished the first corner, he set the tool down and exhaled, not from relief, but recognition.

This was the work that had waited for him.
Not because it needed him.
Because he had finally become someone who could stay.

He walked back to the house, stepping into a living room that held its imperfections without apology. A plant leaned toward the window, slightly off center, reaching for light it never fully received. He crouched beside it and turned the pot gently, adjusting its angle by just enough.

Not dramatic.
Just care.

He watered it slowly, watching the soil darken and take what it needed. The room felt different when he stood again, not brighter and not softer, just honest.

He opened the window a few inches. Fresh air slipped inside, carrying the quiet promise of a world that would meet him exactly where he stood.

This life did not demand greatness from him.
It asked for presence.
And for the first time, he had enough of himself to give it.

Later, he walked to the hill overlooking the town.
The grass bent beneath him. The sky spread wide
above him. Nothing pressed for meaning.

He let the quiet settle.

For once, it did not swallow him.
It steadied him.

Below, the town moved in imperfect rhythms.
People walking. People talking. People leaving and
arriving. Nothing extraordinary. Nothing symbolic.
Just life continuing because life always does.

He felt the shift inside him, subtle and real.
The kind that arrives after truth stops breaking.

Every life he had slipped through had tried to show
him something.
Only this life asked him to stay.

He stood slowly.

The world did not change shape.
The ground did not open.
No version of himself pulled him away.

He walked down the hill with a steadiness he had
never carried before.

The world stayed the same.
He stayed with himself.

And for the first time, that was enough.

He opened the door to his home and stepped inside. The air greeted him with a warmth that asked nothing.

He was not running anymore.
He was not drifting.
He was not searching for the right world to fit inside.

He was choosing the man who would walk through it.

This was the life that would not slip away.
Not because it held him.
Because he finally chose to hold himself.

When the morning opened around him, unpolished and unashamed, Kai walked into it without fear.

The world did not shift this time.
He did.

He had traveled through every version of himself to learn the simplest truth of all: the life he wanted began the moment he stopped leaving it.

Author's Note

I wrote this story to explore a simple idea that often gets lost in the noise of real life.

Most people believe clarity comes from finding the right path.
I have learned that clarity only comes from choosing the version of yourself willing to walk it.

Kai moved through many lives, but each life was only a mirror. Every world showed him something he avoided, forgot, or abandoned in himself. The lesson was never about escape or reinvention. It was about return. It was about learning how to stay.

This book is not about alternate realities.
It is about the quiet truth we meet when we stop running from our own.

If the story leaves you with anything, I hope it is this. The life you want does not appear when everything makes sense. It begins when you choose to show up for the person you are becoming. The shift is never in the world. The shift begins in you.

Thank you for reading.

Acknowledgements

This book was written in the spaces most people
never see.
The quiet moments.
The unfinished days.
The questions stayed longer than the answers.

To everyone who has ever rebuilt themselves in
silence: thank you for giving this story a place to
land. Your resilience shaped the rhythm of this book
more than anything I could write.

To the people in my life who held space for me
while I learned how to stay. You taught me that
presence is not a performance. It is a promise.

To the readers who chose this book from all the
noise in the world. Thank you for trusting me with
your time. Thank you for meeting Kai where he was
and walking with him toward who he became.

And to anyone who is still figuring out how to hold
their own life without running from it: you are not
behind. You are becoming. Stay long enough to see
what that means.

About the Author

Brian B. Turner writes stories for people who are rebuilding.
His work explores the quiet spaces between identity and responsibility, the weight of becoming someone different, and the truth people discover when all the noise finally fades.

He writes from the belief that transformation is not a single moment. It is a series of choices that begin the day a person stops abandoning themselves. His books blend emotional honesty, psychological depth, and spiritual clarity, offering readers a place to breathe and a place to grow.

When he is not writing, Brian builds companies, mentors creators, and studies the way people change when their world no longer fits who they are becoming. His mission is simple. To help people see themselves clearly enough to choose a life they can stay inside.

A Note on What Comes Next

Every story opens a door.
This one opened two.

Kai's journey was about learning to stay.
The next story is about what happens once a person finally does.

The world he chose will not be perfect.
It will not be easy.
But it will be real, and real life always asks a deeper question:

What do you build once you stop running from the person you are becoming?

The next book will explore that question from a different angle.
A new character.
A new struggle.
Another quiet world where the truth rises slowly until it cannot be ignored.

This story ends with a man choosing himself.
The next will begin with someone learning what that choice costs.

Thank you for turning the page with me.

www.ingramcontent.com/pod-product-compliance
Lightning Source LLC
Chambersburg PA
CBHW051343020726
47501CB00007B/2244